Barley

Maria Ruth Murphy

First printed in Great Britain in 2019 by Ragged Butterfly Publishing
A Ragged Butterfly company

First published in paperback in 2019

ISBN: 9781079149050

For my dad, on his 60th birthday,
who gave me the idea for this book.

Chapter 1
Origins
Barley:

There's Archie's da over there gein him a hard time again. Not working hard enough apparently, got his heid in the clouds. Blah, blah. That's just parents for ye. As far as I can see, oor Archie's a grafter. He tends these fields day in, day oot. Well, on the summer holidays anyway. Even if it's baltic, even if it's raining, he's still here looking after those big beasts. And the stench coming aff they animals is atrocious. Bloody shame for him.

Ma mammy gees me a hard time, but I just sling her a deif ear. She says that I speak too much slang. She thinks that members of the 'Golden Promise' family ought to know better. Ma name's Barley by the way and I'm a grain. Ma family is massive; there's hunners of us, with more appearing year after year. We're big time. Team handed. So that gets a lot of respect around here, obviously. Mammy tells me I ought to keep a cool head. She tells me not to be such a wee thug; that I can go places with my life. I just want to be oot of this field, away from these other weans. They do my nut in! The Optics are always putting their big neb in, and the Chariots act like they own the place. Well in my mind Optics sit back and watch other people have fun and Chariots are just there to carry folk. Too soft. I'm no carrying anybody. I'm a grafter like oor Archie, and if you're no up for it, I'll be leaving ye behind. That's the nitty gritty.

Well, would you listen to him? Archie's da, gein it big licks so he is. Just listen.

'Archie, this place disnae run itself. You think you're hard done by, try coming into the distillery and actually using your brains for once.'

The big man's no happy! He's got that look on his face that ma da had when I was cheeky to the other grains. They live on the other side of the field. A right seedy bunch by the way. Mostly buckwheat and rye, but they say they know a few big corns, so I probably shouldnae have opened my mouth.

'I'm no stupit, Da. I'm sure I'd be able.'

Aw naw Archie! Don't you roll your eyes. That's a recipe for disaster!

'Aye well, I'm sick of your attitude. It stinks worse than the sheep. You're taking this life you've got for granted. You cannae just coast through, dreaming and writing in your wee notebook. You need to work hard.'

Archie does work hard. I think that's a bit uncalled for big guy. Look at him, petted lip aboot to greet like a big wean! It's bad enough he's ginger, without you picking on him. I think ye hurt his feelings there, so ye did.

'You're bloody seventeen, Archie, time to man up and start taking a bit of responsibility about this place. I'm not going to be fit forever so, it's time you started learning the trade. I was out grafting at your age.'

Och see! There Da's softened a wee bit, putting an arm round Archie. Must have known he'd went a bit far there with the lecture. I hope this disnae mean I won't see Archie in the field anymore. The pair of them are heading back to the hoose. Enid's probably got them a nice wee stew fixed.

I like it best when Archie comes oot into the field after dinner, before the stars come oot. I love it when he reads to us. He's always got his heid stuck into some book. I see him scribbling in his own notebook sometimes and often wonder what he's writing aboot. That's them oot of sight now, and the sun is sneaking doon behind the hills. There's a pleasant wee breeze picking up, and I love when it sends me bandying about.

The sky looks amazing. Just think, they bastardin' birds get to fly about in it all day. Naw Mammy, I never said a bad word! Ears like a hawk that yin. Glad that mad scarecrow is keeping them at bay. I remember when the gale blew him doon not that long ago. What an absolute blood bath. We were alright, but many a husk has been buried in an unmarked grave here. Archie sorted that though. That scarecrow's not coming doon for anything short of a hurricane. See. That's oor Archie. He's a problem solver, like myself.

Ma mammy insists I'll grow up to be a fine whisky one day. I hope so. I just want more than this. I've grown as much as I can here, and I sometimes feel a bit like I'm in limbo. All this philosophising gets ye sleepy. I'm going for a wee kip under the big lights. Och, I suppose it's not so bad here. It's my home and I'm safe. I'm only a wean after all. There's still plenty of time for growing up.

Chapter 2
The Harvest
Barley:

Whit's that? Whit's that Mammy? Whit dae ye mean it's the harvest? Stop screeching Mammy! Stop it, all of ye, calm doon and tell me exactly what that bloody great hunk of metal is rattling towards us. Och I'm no even listening to this guff. Getting cut doon. I'm in ma prime, that will be right. You're aw panic merchants, it's only Archie and his auld man. They look after us. It won't be anything bad if Archie's behind the wheel, he's ma big mate.

'Archie! Archie! You'll need to keep up beside me with the tractor. Pull your bloody finger oot,' Archie's da is shouting. Archie, they blades are looking awfy sharp on that machine. Snip, snip, snipping aw ma pals and swallowing them up. Put an end to this madness for goodness sake.

'Archie! Whit have ye been telt? Keep alongside the harvester!' Da shouts again.

'You dae it then if it's so easy!'

There we are everyone, pandemonium over. Oor Archie's taking a stand for us. He cannae abide by this cruelty ye see. He's a true humanitarian, or grain-iterian I suppose. He's flinging himself out that tractor in protest, and the auld man is away after him.

'Do you take pride in winding me up?' he asks, absolutely beelin.

Hawl you, get your hands aff the scruff of Archie's collar. Da or no da, I'll be telling on ye. That's it, Archie, push him away. Don't let anybody treat ye like that.

'You're just work shy. If your papa could see —'

'Naw Da, I'm no work shy. You're just the worst teacher I've ever met. Ye cannae just shout oot orders at me. It all might seem simple to you, but I'm still learning. You're making me feel…stupit.'

Poor Archie, ye can tell he's trying. Big baggy circles under those blue eyes of his, probably up worrying about it all night. He slept in, as usual, that's why he's aw higgledy-piggledy with his red hair like straw hinging oot a bin. That's the rage leaving his Da's face now, he's not quite as purple I see. He actually looks a bit embarrassed, gutted even.

'I don't mean to make you feel stupit son. I just get a wee bit frustrated. I worry. I'll no be here to keep an eye on you forever,' says Da.

'I don't need you keeping an eye on me Da. Let's just get this finished,' Archie says, calming doon and jumping back on the tractor.

There's a loud grumble again and the blood bath continues. Da's harvester attacks the field and spits the remains out to Archie's tractor. All my pals are getting mowed down by this creature and sucked into its jaws. It's inches from me now. I look back to my mammy and da. I can see them breaking their hearts. Their only wean is being eaten by a combine harvester. I'm right in front of it now. The reaper has come for me. I'm sorry for being a wee ned Mammy. I cannae look. Aaaarrggh!

That was a wee bit nippy. Something's just sliced through the bottom of me, ripping me from the ground. There's no screaming anymore. Is this the end? Surely heaven's more exciting than this? It's quite dark and hot and I'm being churned around like I'm riding a corkscrew. It's gein me the boke. Excuse me, Archie? Can you please stop this thing? There's a strong chance I'm gaunae whitey. Please pal! Woah, haud on a wee minute. Now I'm slipping aff this corkscrew! I'm holding onto the edge for ma dear life. Maybe I'll just lie low here until Archie comes to his senses. Just hang on tight, Barley boy, hold your grip. Ouch! Ye wee bandit! The rest of them are all flying down on top of me, battering my heid as they fall doon into that big drum. I'm adjusting to the darkness. The last dafty just belted me hard. I'm hanging on by a thread. I look down into the great big drum of doom. The horror unfolds. Poor wee plants are being shaken viciously; it's shaking the very life out of them. They're being rattled about so violently that all their grains fall off leaving only empty sheaths. The sheaths lie there like skeletons, forgotten. This ride is now officially a haunted house. Please let me oot Archie! I cannae take it any longer. Aw naw! Cramp. I'm cramping up! The corkscrew is slipping from my grasp. And down I fall.

IIIIITTTT'SS REEEAALLY NNOOO THHHATT BBBBAAAAAAD GUUUUYYS!
NOOOOO SOOORE JUST A BIIIIT DISORIENTATING.
I FEEEL ALL LOOSE AND LIIIIGHT.

They've shaken my sheath away. Now I'm just a wee grain slipping through a big sieve. Me and all the other wee grains look back up longingly at oor auld bodies. Suddenly they're weeched away oot of sight. They better be treating them with respect.

'Aye right, they use aw that for animal bedding. They let the horses shite all over it.'

That was ma wee pal, Hoppo, sitting beside me in the tank. It's awfy cramped in here. Still, at least we're at the

10

top. There's hunners of wee guys trapped beneath us. Cannae even hear what they're saying under there.

'Probably saying please don't fart!' says ma wee mate Hoppo. I can tell we'll have good banter together.

Cannae believe I thought I was going to die. What a riddy. It disnae look like my mammy and da are coming though. So, a guess that means I won't see them again eh? I'm on my own. I cannae get the image of ma wee mammy crying oot ma heid. Nobody wants to see their wee mammy cry. Now I've started. Big, bold Barley of the field, greeting like a wee wean in front of ma new pals. Archie. If you can hear me, I'm really scared. I don't know why you've done this. Maybe you could let me and Hoppo go home? I just wish I could go home to ma mammy.

Chapter 3
The Spa
Barley:

After aw that greeting, I knew deep down that Archie would see us alright. Me and Hoppo are chilling with the rest of the squad. I still miss ma wee mammy, but I'm buzzing aboot the luxury of this place. Maybe Mammy and Da are on the next machine. I didnae even get a chance to say goodbye. We were chauffeured to the silos and then taken from there into this lovely big bath. This makes up for the hard time they gave us back there. We've just been soaking here, nice and warm.

'But Da, I'm gubbed now. Do I really need to do this as well?'

'You're no at the spa Archie. There's naebody to paint your nails here.'

I beg to differ auld yin. I'm sure there must be some sort of treatment menu, we're having a rare time, so we are Hoppo?

'Aye, Barley mate, I feel years younger.'

That's it, Archie, of course you've triggered another lecture. Everyone let's do a slow clap for Archie.

'Look. To run a business, you must know all the ins and oots of it,' says Da spreading his hands out wide as he explains. 'You need tae know each of your employee's responsibilities and be able to dae it for yourself. How can ye train people, or earn their respect if ye don't know what yer talking aboot? A great leader must be able to put themselves in their followers' shoes.'

'Aye, ok Mufasa,' larks Archie, as he watches us swirl hypnotically in the bubbles.

You might have muttered it. But we all heard it Archie. Getting lippy with the auld man. Will ye never learn?

'Lions don't wear shoes ya dumplin,' Archie's da says, grabbing playfully on the back of his neck. Archie squirms before Da releases him.

'If you're no interested in learning, the stables are needing mucked out,' Da warns.

'Point taken Da.'

'Now that you've finished whinging, I'll explain,' says Da laughing to himself. 'These big tubs,' he says slapping the side of the tub to make a metallic twang, 'are called the barley steeps. It's pretty self-explanatory why, we steep the harvested barley in here.'

'How long is this going to take?' says Archie yawning, rudely.

'Three days.'

'What?' says Archie, ready to hit the roof.

'You'll no be here the full three days son; I'm just trying to get you a taste for the process.'

Archie slumps down onto the bench, and I can just see the enthusiasm ripping right oot of him.

'How come your no having to monitor this aw day?' he asks huffily, flicking through his phone.

'I've done my steeping days son,' Da says swiping the phone from him, 'so just you get on with it wide-o.'

Before all hell can break loose, in walks that big torn-faced clown Dave.

'Arthur,' he says in his monotone drawl, 'the accountant's up at the office for ye. Will I tell him yer busy?'

'Naw, I'll just be up,' Da says to Dave, with a wee nod to dismiss him. 'Get him sorted with a cuppa,' he says, and Dave does the off. Nobody wants to look lazy in front of Da. I wouldn't want to get on his bad side. What a presence he is, by the way. 6ft 4 and as bald as a baby. Still a handsome old man mind. Eh… did I just say that? Maybe it's too hot in this steep and it's all going to ma heid.

'I've got to go see to this Archie,' he says pocketing the phone, 'all you need to know is that the barley will absorb water throughout this process. Then on the third day it will have sufficient moisture levels for germination. So just stay here and keep an eye.'

Archie nods, he looks gutted to be without his phone for the rest of the day. Da leaves him now to his own devices.

Poor Arch. He looks awfy sore and tired as he's stretching oot all his muscles. He's parking his bum now for a rest. Quite right mate. After all, we're chilling in the bath, you should too. He's pulling a book out his overalls. *The Great Gatsby* it says. Like I told ye, he's always got his nose in a book this yin. Looks a bit eerie to me, with a pair of big eyes watching oot of the cover. But I do love to listen to Arch read. He likes to read the dialogue out loud, and he begins rhyming some off now.

'You're a lovely reader.'

Weet wheel! Now, now Archie, don't get a beamer. The most beautiful lassie has just popped her head round the door. Must be the new bird I've heard them all talking about. She's got her long brown hair tied back in a ponytail, with a fringe threatening to fall into her green eyes. Archie's went from flushed to Casper in twenty seconds.

'Och, I didnae think anyone was listening,' he says with a big smile.

I've got to hand it to him, he does sound quite casual. But I know Archie, and his heart is probably going tackety boots like mine. She's a stunner.

'Your ma sent these for ye,' she says as she hands Archie his sandwiches. Ha! Ha! Well done Archie's mammy, embarrassing the wean in front of the new bird. That's what I like to see. Classic. Wow, with that smile she's got, she could light up the whole distillery. Archie doesn't say anything as he takes the pieces. He just shakes his head, thinking of his wee mammy fondly. She's always mothering him, even though he's seventeen and a big lump.

'It's nice to see a young guy who reads, Arch,' Alice says, sitting down beside him. She picks up the book, smoothing it out.

'I love it,' he says, 'helps you get out of this place.'

'It's not so bad here surely?' Alice says sincerely.

'Well, it's getting better,' Archie replies with that big smile again. What a charmer. His mammy's telt him he's got a good smile so he's showing it off like naebody's business. Well in, Arch. There she's grinning again, with that gorgeous smile.

'You should read *The Beautiful and Dammed*. I'd give you *my* copy, but the state of this book I'd never let you near it,' Alice says tapping him on the head with the ratty book. 'You should stick to kindle.'

'And have you knock me out with it?' he says, playfully wrestling it out of her hands. 'I like my books to look read Alice. It's no been enjoyed if its spines no broke and it's no got half a dozen tea stains on it,' he says laughing.

'And here I thought you were a gentleman Arch,' she says, before looking at her watch. 'Oh sugar! That's my break just about done. I've got to get back to the still house before James goes mental.'

Alice starts making her move towards the door.

'Did ye come down here on your break just for me?' Archie asks, flattered.

Now she's blushing. Oh, how the tables have turned.

'Aw it was nothing,' she says sweeping the fringe from her eyes, 'your ma asked when I was up at the canteen. I didn't mind.'

'Well, I appreciate that,' Archie says, flashing her that winning grin again.

She nods and gives a small wave before leaving. Archie heaves a big sigh and slumps down to his previous slobbish posture. It's like he's breathing for the first time. But wait, there's the future Mrs popped her head back in.

'What age are you Archie?' she asks hopefully.

'Me? I'm seventeen,' he replies with a puzzled look, 'eighteen in December.'

Now, I'm not sure why, but for some reason the future Mrs Archie looks awfy disappointed in that.

'Shame. I thought you were my age,' she says cryptically. 'See you later, Archie.'

Before she leaves Archie says something that surprises her.

'Alice...we've all got souls of different ages.'

'You have read it then?' she smiles, hanging on the door.

'Oh, you don't want to see the copy,' he laughs.

'See you later, Archie,' she says as her smile wrinkles her nose. Then she's away down the stairs again.

'A shame?' Archie says, bewildered, when she's gone. She's got him aw messed up now, he disnae know what to think. Alice is nineteen, doing her apprenticeship at the still house from what I've heard the other dafties in this place saying. I can almost see the wee cogs in his head turning.

16

Aye, I think so too Archie. She was wanting to winch ye, but it turns out your too young. Cannae win them all big guy.

'Naw,' says Archie to himself, shaking the idea out of his mind and wolfing down his pieces.

'What's Ma aw aboot sending her down here?' he says, laughing between bites. Well, at least you've still got your mammy, Archie.

'Ye greeting again?' pipes up Hoppo.

Naw Hoppo, sniff, I've just got something in my eye.

Archie's dusting off his hands and is back to watching us bubble in the tub. Archie can't wipe the smirk aff his face. There's Da back.

'Nice to see a man happy at his work,' Da says, confused, but pleased at Archie's attitude for a change. He hands back the phone for good behaviour.

What's that Hoppo? Aye. Ye may just be right. If Archie could get Alice to overlook the age gap, well, he'd defo be in for a winch.

Chapter 4

Germination

Barley:

We've been soaking in this water for three days now. Just when I was thinking, this is too far, the water drains away and we've dropped into the floor below. My main man Archie stoats in. He's got his auld da in tow. Thank god, Archie mate. I was aboot to go mad in here! Hoppo's patter is wearing a bit thin.

'Here you, wrap it!'

I call it like I see it, Hoppo. Anyway, there's only so much ye can soak and I feel aw swollen and bloated. Disnae seem like much of a spa to me. Ye cannae go aboot making people feel fat. It's no good for the self-esteem, Archie.

'Right. Now Archie, we've soaked the barley for 3 days. Ye listening? Gees that phone. Are you this cheeky in school?'

'I am listening Da,' Archie says averting his da's hands and slipping it back into his overalls. He disnae want a repeat of the last time.

'Ye better be Son,' Archie's da takes a breath and goes onto explain slowly. 'We've soaked the Barley and now it's time for the germination stage.'

'A didnae know you knew big words like that,' Archie jokes.

'Cheeky wee bandit!'

Hawl you! I'll not stand by this child cruelty. Cannae just batter him over the heid wae yer paper. There are numbers for that ye know. Archie should phone the RSPCA on ye. Bet that's how ye tried to take his phone.

'That might work if Archie was a Labrador or something,' Hoppo says, slagging me. He knows what I meant.

'Take a joke, sake,' Archie says.

'Do you think this is just some big joke aye? Some laugh running yer ain distillery. I've not a care in the world,' Da says exasperated. Aye Archie. Best keep that motor mouth of yours shut. I can see that angry vein in his head again, and that's never a good sign. Good choice mate.

'Germination, ahem…wipe that smirk aff yer face Archie I'm warning ye. It's where the barley sprouts and becomes the green malt that we need for the next part of the process.'

Eh what? Sprouts? Sounds a bit painful to me, have a word Arch.

'How do we dae that then?' he says, finally perking up.

'That's more like it son, a bit of enthusiasm. What we do is, we transfer the barley to the malting floor. The water was drained from the barley in the last process and the barley now sits in these things above us, the steeps,' Archie's Da says, as they look up to three big, cone-shaped contraptions hanging doon from the ceiling.

'We take the barley from the steeps and we spread it all. We call it casting the steeps.'

Archie looks at the long barn in front of him and then to his fellow workers waiting by the windows to start their shift. Da continues.

'During germination the wee enzymes at work turn the starch in the barley into soluble sugars. That's crucial for when we want to convert them to alcohol later,' he says, pausing to make sure Archie follows ok. We're with ye big man, carry on.

'Then two to three times a day you and the boys are gaunae come in and turn the malt by hand. With these big shovels,' Da explains carefully, lifting a huge shovel for Archie to see.

'By hand? That will be right. I understand the process Da, I don't need to go through all the rigmarole to get it,' Archie says dismissively. He's a big tall lad oor Archie; 6ft 2 and still growing by the looks of it. But there's no much meat on him, and even less muscle I'd say. He'll no cope.

'We turn the barley by hand, because we honour traditional craftsman ship at Ionach distillery, Arch. We like the auld ways, and we think that adds a special character to oor dram. We've aw done it, so now it's your turn. For a full week.'

'The boys can handle it on their own Da, big strapping lads like them. It'll be nae bother,' Archie negotiates.

Archie's da laughs and shakes his head at the other workers waiting nearby for the shift to begin. They chuckle in reply.

'Don't let this wee shite pull the wool over yer eyes boys, he knows how to skive.'

'Right well ok, I'll spread it all out on the malting floor. But how can we no just leave it there to germinate or whatever?'

'Need to make sure it doesn't get mouldy son, only way to do that is to make sure the malt gets turned frequently. Also, if you leave it too long it can sprout too quickly, and we don't want that. Simple as that.'

Archie's da is just abandoning him now with the other workers.

'Mon,' says Alasdair, signalling Archie to come over to come closer to the end steep. He places a huge wheelbarrow with large disk wheels below the funnel.

'This is the malt chariot. See how it looks like you could attach a horse to it?' He slides a large disk that traps the grain aside to fill the chariot and Archie follows him as he barrels it out onto the floor. Archie and the other boys rake out the big piles he leaves behind. I can already see Archie knackered.

The boys go for a break and come back when it's time for the first turning. That big, handsome lout Hamish just handed Archie a big malt shovel. I can tell there's some weight in it 'cause Archie's skinny arms faltered when he took it.

'This isnae really a job for a wee wean, but yer da insists,' Hamish says with a big smile on his face. What a big, smug bastard. You're a man now Archie, nearly eighteen. Don't take that shite fae him. Even if his heid's the size of a big bowling ball and he's got hands the size of that shovel. Well, that's not what really matters in life. It's all about how you handle yourself intellectually; the old grey matter. There you can best him, Arch. He probably cannae even spell shovel. You could write a book about one.

'The incredible adventures of Shovel!'

Och, wheesht Hoppo, naebody's laughing.

'Whit age are you anyway?' asks Archie, looking at him and sizing him up as they begin turning the malt. I mean Hamish is obviously an idiot, but he's a big solid guy. It would be daft to say Archie didn't envy the physique in some way. He's what you'd want to be when you really grow up, but probably less of a twat.

'30, and far too old to be babysitting,' Hamish sneers back.

'Well I'm no a wean. I'm just here to learn all the bits of the distillery. So I can see who the weaklings are when I take over.'

Ha! Ha! Classic, Archie ma man. That'll put his gas at a peep. Look at him and his big monkey shoulders.

'Nae bother "boss". In the meantime, get shovelling,' Hamish demands, undaunted. He's laughing at Archie as he walks away to the other end of the malting floor. He's telling all the other malt-men what he said. Chump.

Chapter 5
The Kiln
Barley:

I'm not going to lie to ye, I'm feeling aw oot of sorts. Hoppo too, and the rest of the grains it seems. I've sprouted. I've got wee hairy roots now and I even feel like my voice is deeper. I don't feel like myself anymore. A full week they left us oot on that malting floor, aw exposed. It was damp, but nice and warm in there at least or we'd have a caught oor death. A couldnae even just go for a nice long kip, coz every time I managed to doze off that big smug monkey shoulder bastard would start turning us over again. He made poor Arch do most of the back-breaking work, the swine. I'm telling ye, his card is marked when the big man takes over. Just you wait and see. Anyways, a full week a being tossed and turned. I thought they might be doing the same the day, but something's obviously different today. Maybe its cause we've aw sprouted? Too feart to mess with us now maybe? We're being loaded up and taken over to the kiln elevator, whatever that means?

'They're going to burn us!' Hoppo squeals. Will you stop panicking. They are not going to burn high quality, germinated malt like oorselves. The elevator is in a two-story building with a roof that's shaped like a Buddhist temple. I wonder if this is the meditation area. Before the workers send us up, we get a chance to see Da and Archie talking beside what looks like a big oven.

'Now this is the kiln room,' I hear Da explaining.

'I know Da,' Archie yawns, 'dead giveaway the big kiln and the sign saying, *Kiln Room*.'

'Look, when your teaching someone it's always best to assume they know nothing. Look up Socrates if you're so clever. So, you were right when you said I make you feel stupit the other day. It's probably the best way to teach. Treat everyone like an idiot and they'll never get lost. I'm telling ye it aw fae scratch.'

'Stinks!' Archie moans, pulling his overall collar over his nose.

'That's the peat reek son. See that black earthy type stuff?'

'Aye?'

'That's peat. Over the years in Scotland, plants and trees and all sorts of greenery gets compressed into the earth and forms this substance. We're lowland, so we don't traditionally use peat in our drying process but I'm wanting to try something different since this is your first barrel we're producing,' Da explains.

'Do we no need to stick to the same formula every time?' Archie asks, 'I thought we were all about the tradition here at Ionach.'

'Naw! Technically, we can do what we want son. And I think it's maybe about time the distillery started doing things a bit differently,' he assures.

'Is that what the accountant said Da?' Archie asks nosily.

'Just never you mind what the accountant said. Try and listen and learn a bit.'

Archie nods, he obviously knows that's no an issue to push further with Da.

'When we dry the grains, by toasting them in here, it halts the germination process. It's gone as far as we want it to now. Ye see that we're on two levels. The heat and peat smoke ascend into the floor above. The grains are dried until crisp and the peat will impart a smoky flavour into the whisky.'

'I widnae know anything about the taste of whisky Da,' says Archie, cheekily.

'Aye,' says Da, 'you keep sneaking whisky fae my stash and you'll end up as bald as me, I promise.' Archie raises his eyebrows, he's no falling for that one, he's no ten.

'I'm no kidding son, it'll rob the hair fae yer heid and put it here,' he's opening his shirt to reveal a big hairy chest and laughing like a big friendly giant. Now Archie's Da's phone is ringing.

'Hello!' he says in his deep tone. 'What? Right... just stay with her till I get up there. Cheers.' Archie's da looks dazed as he buttons up his shirt again. I can tell me and Arch are both wondering what the script is here.

'I'm going to have to leave you to your own devices now son,' he says distantly as he fumbles around looking for his glasses and keys.

'When will ye be back?' Archie asks worried. He's no exactly experienced here, it's a bit overwhelming.

'I'm no sure. Any problems find Dave,' Da says, referring to his assistant distillery manager.

'What's wrong Da?' Archie probes further, to which Da waves a big hand his way.

'Look, don't worry just get that malt dried,' he says as he sweeps out of the kiln room, like a man on a mission.

Archie looks awfy worried. I would be too. If it's not meetings with the accountants, it's his da running off oot of the blue. Who was he talking aboot? Archie's wise enough to know it's just something he can't control, so he'll just need to put it oot of his mind.

'Right, let's get this rattled,' he says to himself, throwing himself into the task. Shovel by shovel he stocks the kiln oven with coke and peat. I'm toasting away here in the room above. This would be magic if it wasn't for that horrible stench. Archie wipes his sweaty brow and puts on his mask.

'Bit better he mumbles,' as he shovels more into the kiln.

We've been spread out along this floor above him. Asides from the room slowly filling with smoke and clouding my vision, it's quite pleasant here. This is like the days being oot in the sun in the field, so warm. I wonder how my mammy and da are. I hope the sun is still shining on them, wherever they may be.

Chapter 6
True Grist
Barley:

Wheeee! We're flying down a wee chute and into the malt hopper. Woooooaaaah! We're being jiggled about again. Where are we going Hoppo?

'The mill!' he yells. You don't need to sound so feart I'm sure it will be fine.

'Right, after the kiln, the dried malt has been put through the malt hopper and then passes through into the malt mill. This big lump of machinery basically just grinds and chops up the grain inside till it's finer,' says Archie's da, looking up at the big red machine. What the fu... no Archie! Grind? Chop? Your old pal Barley? Surely noooot! Help! We're dropping into the mill and the teeth are coming towards us. It's excruciating, as I'm being battered and bitten by this beast. Come on then, square go! Give it yer best shot. I'm Barley Golden Promise. You'll never crush my spirit.

'So, you're just operating the machine and monitoring the progress,' Da explains.

'The grist gets transferred via they big pipes into the mash house for the next bit of the process. Do you understand so far?'

'Aye, it's pretty self-explanatory. It's no really a hands-on part of the process is it?' Archie confirms.

'Nah, it's easy. I can feel confident just leaving you to it.'

'Sound, Da,' Archie smiles.

'Nice to see you enjoying it a bit more. It's actually very interesting isn't it?'

'Maybe, but I think the actual distilling has got to be the best part.'

'All in good time son,' says Da knowingly, 'Get this done and tomorrow I'll introduce ye to the mash tun.' Da makes his way oot of the room, bumping into Alice as she enters. He does a double take as he walks away, probably wondering why the still house apprentice is bringing pieces to his boy.

When Archie sees the future Mrs, wow, his face lights up. Try not to seem too keen big man, you'll scare her off. She's waving the pieces in her hand.

"Your mammy sent these down again," she says, flashing that lovely smile.

"Aw cheers, Alice you're a wee star," Archie says, 'Do you want to share them with me? Seems like she's made extra?'

'Trying to set us up do you think?' Alice says laughing.

'She's got good taste in women I'd say,' Archie shrugs.

'It wouldn't work Archie, I'm too old for you,' Alice dismisses, sitting down and tearing one of the pieces in half.

'Your only two years older Alice, it's no exactly grab a granny!'

Alice is knotted in laughter, covering her mouth as she laughs.

'Why do ye hide yer mouth when ye laugh Alice?'

'Oh, I really hate my smile. I always got called Gnasher in school, and whenever I laughed the pelters would get worse,' she says wolfing down half of the sandwich.

'What? You've got the best smile I've ever seen!' says Archie, unconvinced. 'And you're always smiling for me.'

'I can't help it round about you Arch,' she says locking eyes with him.

'Anyway, years of braces has made my teeth better, but I don't think I'll ever get over hiding them when I laugh,' she confesses. 'If I don't, I feel like they're sitting in my mouth two sizes two big.'

'Bet ye were stunning even with braces. Bet they only wound ye up cause they fancied ye,' Archie guessed. 'I can't image anyone who wouldn't.'

'No,' Alice replies, blushing, 'I never even had a boyfriend in school, I was far too geeky.'

I cannae imagine any man that wouldn't want a date with Alice. I mean she's a different species to me and I'd still fire in. Archie's certainly taken with her.

'If your hinting, I've already told you I'll take you out, Alice.'

'I think your brilliant, but really I think there's too much of an age gap. You're not even allowed in the pubs yet; I'd look like a bit of a creep!' she warns. Something in her tone tells me she's finding it hard to justify her excuse to herself. There might be hope yet Arch.

'Fair enough, but age is just a number. I'm sure I could get into the pub no bother if you wanted me to take you. I'm bulking out a bit these days,' Archie says subtly flexing his arms.

'You are Archie, any girl *your* age would be lucky to have you,' she says, playfully pinching his stomach.

'Nothing to stop ye being my pal though is there? Or are ye setting an age limit on that too?' Archie grins.

'Aye, a pal sounds good. Your great company anyway,' Alice says leaning into him, fondly. There's that laugh again, it's pure heaven.

'I'll take you out as a pal then, tonight if you're free?' Archie says, trying to hide his excitement.

'Sounds good to me. I'm in cottage 3, you can pick me up after my shift tonight,' she replies. Alice is looking a bit flushed. She's getting up and brushing the crumbs off her overalls.

'Thanks for sharing your pieces,' she says as Archie stands up to face her. He's so much taller than her. They're awfy close now. Is it time for the winch maybe? He's slipping his hands into hers. Och, just get on with it will ye!

They're both looking at their hands entwined. This is a bit too cosy for pals surely? He kisses her on the forehead and grabs her in for a hug.

'Shame it's not a height restriction for dating you, then I'd do alright wee yin,' he teases. She bats him in the stomach and pushes him away.

'See you tonight *pal*,' she says and then she's gone. Archie sighs into the air, looking at the door she's just left by. He reaches into his overall pockets for his notebook. He's probably writing her some love poem the big sap. Haud on a minute! What's that noise? We're moving again. Fast this time, through a pipe and away from Archie. Before I go, I hear John come in with a wheel barrel and say something to Archie.

'Archie, you'll need to go and collect the horse droppings.'

'What?' Archie asks, bewildered.

'Aye, I'm sure your da meant to say. A barrelful from the stable. We need it for the mash house process.' He says it so deadpan. I would believe it, but I'm not a complete dafty. No, Archie, don't be so stupit. It's a wind up. Archie. Archie. Don't you dare take that wheel barrel. Before I can see what he does, I'm whisked away. I hope he didn't fall

30

for that. A barrel full of horseshit? This boy is meant to be clever, what does he think they'll use that for? It's gein me the boke thinking of it. We're rattling through the pipe now, rapid. I don't know where we're going, Hoppo. But we'll survive whatever. If we've proven anything, it's that we've got true grist.

Chapter 7
The Mash Tun
Barley:

It turns oot the pipe funnelled us into a big metal hot tub. It's roasting hot and we're all sitting stewing. We're in the mash tun, and the humid air fills the room. There's a funny earthy smell all around. Probably the rest of these smelly rats in here. Know what I mean Hoppo? It's not exactly V.I.P. They must not know who I am. I can see Archie and Da through the opening in the tub.

'So, what are you doing about uni then?' Da asks, with arms folded after a big sigh.

'We had to apply, it wisnae even an option not to Da. But nobody asked me if I even want to go. It was just assumed,' Archie says mirroring his da's pose and leaning against the railing.

'Well you've obviously got it son. That's no small thing. These teachers know the people that can do it and the people that can't,' Da says proudly, a big grin spreading across his face.

'I just told you, everyone basically got forced into it,' Archie says, brushing off the praise. I tell ye Hoppo, he disnae actually believe how clever he is. Well, book smart I'd say after that shit shovelling incident. Showed yourself up wae that one Arch.

'Aye, you and aw your wee brainy pals more like. I'm sure there's folk in that school that would love to have that assumption made about them,' Da says, and he's definitely getting ready for a lecture. Cannae be bothered with this, maybe I'll try get a wee snooze in here. Archie is silent and listening, but you can tell he thinks Da disnae really know anything about school.

'What I mean Arch, is you're mixing with the clever ones. There are people there who want to do it, and try hard, but they'd be lucky to get a labouring apprenticeship somewhere,' Da explains. 'I'm speaking from experience; some things just hold ye back and ye get written off by the teachers.'

Archie tries to squirm away from the subject, avoiding Da's eyes and examining oor hot tub intensely. He knows it's no going to work.

'Well, I've applied, but I don't know what I'll do,' Archie says defensively. He's rolling his shoulders and cricking his neck. That wilnae get Da aff yer back Archie.

'Where did you apply?' says Da, unwilling to drop the issue.

'Glasgow, St. Andrew's and Dundee. Like I said. I might not even get in,' Arch replies huffily.

'Listen, if you get yer grades and a letter in saying your accepted, *take* the place. Get the heid doon and do it,' Da advises, as it's clearly a no-brainer for him.

'What's the point Da? I want to take over this place eventually,' Archie says, sounding more like a whiney child than a future business owner. Da sighs, shaking his head in exasperation.

'Do you know what I would have done to have school come as easy as it does to you? I was clever, still am mind, but some things I just couldn't get. I got given a fitbaw and told to go play ootside,' Da laughs recalling it. 'Actually, I remember one day just sitting there and realising I couldn't keep up. Dyslexia. So, I asked for the fitbaw. I took myself out of the equation.'

'I bet you were still shite at fitbaw though,' teases Archie.

'Better than you'll ever be,' Da replies in good sprit, but the serious tone still floats in the air.

'Look at me now. I'm a grafter and always has been. That's how I've done all this. And most importantly I'm driven to look after my family and give you everything you deserve,' he says grabbing Arch by the shoulders.

'You deserve to know that you've done it. Gave it your best shot with no regrets. Just think where I might have been had I stuck in,' he says.

'You're doing alright Da,' says Archie looking all around room, but Da's not having any of it.

'Don't aim for mediocrity son. That's no the boy I raised,' he warns. 'Look my advice is, if you get in, then do a year at least and see if you do well. If you despise it after a year, just sit your exams and come home. You'll have finished the modules and got something at least. You'll know it wisnae for you after all. What's the harm?'

'I just don't want to waste four years of my life on something I'm not sure about,' Archie explains, coming clean to Da.

'Archie, learning is never a waste. Aye you might never use your degree for what it's designed for. So what?' Da says trying to rally him.

'It's learning skills and dealing wae situations, and people, you would never encounter otherwise. People ye'd never meet in this wee toon. It's deadlines, time management and work ethic. It's group work with fannies with dreadlocks and medallions that you wouldn't give the time of day at home son. It's making lifelong friends wae they fannies and changing your whole personality and outlook on life,' Da waxes on.

34

'Does that no sound smashing?'

'You sound like a prospectus,' Archie jokes but I can tell he's starting to warm to the big man's idea. He does sell it well. Do you think I could maybe go with him Hoppo?

'They don't take numpties, Barley mate, sorry.'

'It's doing fresher's week and living away from your ma for the first time. It's becoming who yer meant to be son. Does that no sound like the right move?' Da continues, but Archie is still arse perched on the fence. He can see he needs more convincing.

'Make me a deal. You get in, then you'll go and try. Cause if you're foolish enough to waste this opportunity, then I don't want you anywhere near my business,' Da says sternly, and it's clear he means every word.

'I think you're getting ahead of yourself Da, like I said, I might not even get in. But if it makes you chill a wee bit then aye, it's a deal,' Archie says, shaking Da's hand.

'But if I do come back and run the business that fud John is for the off!'

'How?' asks Da confused.

'He had me barrelling horse shit for this part of the process. Alice told me it's a lot of shit, literally. But that was after I'd a barrel load,' says Archie raging. Da erupts into hysterical laughter, his big deep laugh is booming and maniacal.

'What do you mean you fell for that? Aw they brains and universities crying out for ye and ye still fell for that! Ya plonker.'

'How am I meant to know? I wisnae sure if was for fertiliser or something,' Archie says defensively.

'Going to uni could be the making of you son. You might not need to come back and deal wae these clowns,'

Da says, still laughing. This seems to be annoying Archie though, maybe he's got a taste for this distilling stuff after all.

'What about you and the business Da? You cannae run it forever.'

'I will, if you don't pull up your socks boy. You don't seem that interested so far. It's not all lording it up over people you know,' Da says. His words look like they've gutted Archie.

'Go to uni son, find out who you are before making me any promises,' Da says, with a large hand on his shoulder, before bringing him over to our big hot tub.

'Right, enough of this uni malarkey. Time for the real learning. This is the mash tun. The grain has been ground down into a fine flour we call *Grist.* That's what you supervised in the malt mill,' Da says, before giving a wee chuckle. 'Until stupit heid sent you on a wild goose chase.'

Archie rolls his eyes and Da continues.

'The grist then gets shunted into this big tub. Just now it's sitting at about sixty-seven degrees Celsius. The water gets added in three stages and reaches almost boiling point. All the while the big paddles inside are mixing it up. Go on, have a look,' encourages Da, pointing at the open window at the top of the tub. Hello Archie!

'It's quite a sweet smell you'll get, if you notice, that's the starch in the grain being converted to sugars,' coaches Da.

Woooosh! More water is added to the tub, and it isn't half getting hotter.

'We begin to produce a sweet liquid called *Wort,* which gets drained off here,' Da says showing Archie the anatomy of it.

'That goes through the pipes and cooling system and is brought back down to twenty degrees before being transferred to the wash house for fermentation. The spent grain left behind is used to feed the coos, so it's an economical by-product that's very beneficial here,' Da explains further. Archie seems to be eating up his every word. I've noticed he's even started writing it in his wee notebook.

'It's so good they say they want mooooooooore,' Da says churning out ultimate cheddar-cheese patter.

'Sorry,' he says, 'that was pish. But a good teacher always uses humour. And I bet you'll still remember that in 20 years.'

Naw big man, I'm struggling to remember it even now. Pure pish. Da shows Archie how they monitor the process and just as he's wrapping up his explanation there's a wee knock on the doorway.

It's Alice again, looking gorgeous as ever. Fancy jumping in the bath darlin? They're calling me *Wort*, but I think that's a bit out of order! I've no got warts I swear. She looks in sheepishly, obviously scared to interrupt.

'Alright Alice, you need to speak to me?' says Archie's Da cheerfully. Both Archie and Alice look a bit awkward.

'Eh no sorry, I was actually just wanting to quickly talk to Archie,' she explains, her cheeks now abloom. 'I'll come back later though, sorry!'

I don't know who looks more embarrassed, Archie's da or oor Alice. A look of realisation filters onto his face. He picks up his glasses and papers and says,

'Och nae bother doll, I thought it was maybe a problem at the still house.' Nicely saved there Da.

'Aye, so Arch, you know what you're monitoring here. Think your due a break anyway, but just keep an eye eh?' Da says with a proud pat on Archie's shoulder.

'Aye Da,' Archie agrees, and I can tell inside he's shouting - *just go Da!* He can take a hint and politely makes himself scarce, leaving Alice to enter the mash house.

Alice hands Archie a plastic tub for his lunch this time.

'Ma's a bit fancy today,' he says, excitedly prising it open to reveal a lovely salad.

'Chicken and chorizo salad with lemon dressing,' Alice explains proudly.

'I thought I'd make your lunch to say thanks for the cinema last night. You didn't need to pay you know.'

Archie is buzzing, no wonder, it looks dynamite. She's ticking aw the boxes if she can cook Arch.

'Looks brilliant Alice, cheers. And it was fair enough, you let us watch that superhero movie. Wisnae exactly yer first choice,' he says picking up the fork and spearing a bit of chicken.

'Och, it's good to branch out,' Alice waves dismissively.

'And it had ye greeting like a chick flick anyway,' Archie teases her.

'Hawl, that was actually a very sad ending! Even the big guy beside me was tearful,' she jokes sidling up closer, to wind him up.

'Naw!' he denies.

'I'm sure I saw a wee twinkle,' she insists, looking into his eyes again.,

'Nah, nah!' he maintains, laughing. 'The jalapenos were just getting to me that's all.'

The way they laugh together, it's brilliant. They've just got that kind of banter that flows and makes you smile to listen.

'So, you just thought ye'd check in on your emotional friend then, aye?' says Archie playing along.

'Oh aye, it's follow-up therapy from your traumatic cinema experience. There really should be a disclosure at the beginning,' Alice laughs and accepts a bit of Chorizo that Archie feeds her off the fork.

'Brilliant isn't it?'

'Mmmm!' she sighs. 'I'm some chef by the way. Anyway, I've got to go. I've got a test today for my apprenticeship, so I've not to take a full break. I'll need to shoot,' Alice pinches another bit of Chorizo.

'Well thanks for looking after me,' Arch says smiling, he's never had a girl make him lunch before. Except for his mammy, and she disnae count.

'Since your ma is a bit under the weather too, I thought. How is she by the way?' asks Alice, making Archie's smile slip. He prods the salad a bit before answering.

'Aye, still feeling rubbish, but I'm sure the doctor will get to the bottom of it.'

Alice nods with a kind smile that makes Archie blurt out more.

'She's a hard wee woman. I'm sure she could batter a guy if she needed to,' he bursts oot laughing, and Alice joins in, but that sad look remains. I think she can see past his humour.

'A bit like yourself Alice. Small but tough,' he continues clearing the lump from his throat with a cough.

'It's a big compliment to be compared to your ma by the way. She's such a lovely person,' Alice says, touched.

'She's always popping down to the canteen to have a wee gossip with me,' she says fondly. Archie gulps, almost choking on his chorizo. What secrets has mammy been spilling?

'Nothing to do with you, don't worry,' she assures as she's leaving. 'Nothing I'll hold against you anyway.' Alice laughs and with a wink she disappears oot of the room. But I reckon she'll not be oot of oor Archie's mind for hours.

Chapter 8

The Wash House

Barley:

'Her? Naw I've already pumped her twice. The wee dirty! She's probably only got the job cause she's banging James in the still house.'

WHALLOP!

Archie's on top him, absolutely smashing his face in. It's sickening, as bone crunches bone. I almost cannae look, there's so much blood. There are other men trying to pull him off, but I think he's actually going to kill the guy. Stop Archie! STOP! He isnae worth it mate.

'Right big man that's enough, he's out cold,' Danny says as he manages, finally, to heave an exhausted Archie off Stevie. He's lying sparkled on the floor in a pool of blood.

'Fucking scum bag! Alice widnae go near ye,' Archie shouts over Danny's arms which separate them.

'Are you fucking crazy? He cannae hear ye. Ye've mashed his face in,' says Henry trying to wake Stevie up. He's wincing at the blood now covering his own overalls.

'Go and sit doon,' demands Danny, panic clear in his voice. Things have escalated quickly. Naebody saw that coming, especially not Stevie.

Reluctantly, Archie's sitting doon now on the steps leading up to the washbacks. His eyes are glaring at the boys helping Stevie. This was quite a nice cosy atmosphere until Archie went ballistic. The *Wort*, as they now call us, is split up over three washbacks. These are massive wooden tubs that half fill the room. They've added yeast to these tubs. We're fermenting, you see. There's a musty scent in the air and you need to be careful not to take a big breath near the washbacks as the process produces a hell of a lot of CO_2. Could knock out a horse Archie's Da has said. Well, Archie's knocked out a donkey all in his own by the looks of it.

The boys are trying to wake the clown up. Archie sits with his head in his hands, with burst and bloodied knuckles. But they're not a patch on this guy's coupon.

'Fuck sake Archie, this is serious! I think you've burst his eye socket,' Danny says, lifting a swollen eyelid to see his pupils.

'We need to phone an ambulance, Danny,' panics Henry as he fumbles for his phone. Archie shoots up, rage controlling him again. Calm doon Archie.

'Whit? Just get him woken up and to first aid. He deserved a tanking for speaking that way!' he snarls, the consequences of his actions clearly bubbling into his mind now. Squeaky bum time, I think.

'You could get the jail for this if he presses charges,' one of then warns. Archie tries to look unbothered, but I can tell he's already planning an escape to Mexico before Da finds oot.

'Go and get Arthur and then meet the ambulance at the front of distillery. They'll not know their way around here,' Henry says as he dials 999. Danny literally runs out of the wash house to find him.

I can hear Henry explaining it all to the operator. A violent assault.

'Assault? A lot of pish!' defends Archie, 'It was a square go, he should have defended himself.'

Henry looks at him in annoyance, struggling to hear the operator. He's checking breathing again now. He's pulling up the eyelid that's not swollen up to the size of an orange. Aw naw Archie, this is serious mate! Henry's off the phone now. He's aw peely-wally.

'Go and wash your hands,' he commands in a cool voice.

'Get the first aid box and bandage them. We cannae have you contaminating the product.' As Henry speaks, he's gathering his things to leave.

'You need to stay here and man the fort. You cannae touch the floor when he's gone, the police might need to see that.'

'What do you mean the police might need to see it?' says Archie defensively.

'That's evidence,' says Henry snidely. He is one of Stevie's pals, so I'm not surprised.

'I'm no putting my arse on the line for you, turning a blind eye while ye destroy it,' he says, with a sort of laughing sneer.

'You need to stay here. I'm going to need to write up a report of this disaster for Dave, and the police if needs be.'

'I don't think it needs to go as far as all that,' Archie says, trying to save his own arse.

'Assault on a fellow employee! It's a fucking nightmare for you *and* your da. I don't want tarnished with this for no writing the report,' he says, looking at Archie with contempt.

'You're meant to have brains Arch. What were you thinking? This could be your life over,' he says, but his words hold only jealousy and not real concern.

Danny's back now with the ambulance crew, just as Stevie starts to twitch back to consciousness on the floor.

He's disorientated and they hoist him onto a stretcher. He looks a pathetic, blood-soaked mess as they carry him away. The female paramedic looks at Archie's bloodied hands with disgust. He immediately makes his way to the washing up area, cleaning and bandaging his hands. He winces. They are bruising up and look like the bone might be trying to burst through the skin.

Slam! The door rattles on its hinges as Archie's Da's comes barrelling in. He's fuming. Absolutely, fuming.

'Right, I need to write the report up for this *incident* chief, and speak to Dave,' says Henry.

'I am a witness,' he says, in attempt to appear impartial. But I know he's desperate to dob oor Archie in and make his slime ball pal look like the victim. Grass-bag.

'Go ahead,' Da says, not even looking at him. He's shooting straight towards Arch in the small cloakroom. Da grabs him by the collar and yanks him towards his face. His teeth are gritted in anger.

'What the fuck Archie!' he growls, before pushing him roughly away, leaving Archie to catch his balance. I can tell it's taking aw his da's strength not to batter him the now.

'I'm sorry, Da, I just lost it,' Arch says, tracing the bandages of his left hand.

'Lost it? That boy's in a bad way Archie. Stretchered out of here. Out of my distillery!' Da explodes, his big bald heid completely beetroot with high blood pressure.

'He was saying horrible things about Alice—'

'Don't you fucking *dare* utter one more word!' Da warns, as the Alice excuse disnae wash. 'I don't want to know what pathetic excuse you've got,' says Da and Archie shrinks down.

'If my employee, presses charges you'll be in big bother. The police might even be involved already. I'm supposed to be keeping my employees safe, no scraping them up off the distillery floor,' he rants. 'It's a whole shit show, Archie, and you're centre stage!'

Da paces up and down rubbing his bald heid, deep in thought. Maybe if ye rub it hard enough a genie will appear and sort aw this oot. Archie is watching Da silently like a naughty puppy.

'I thought I was doing the right thing giving you a chance to be a part of this,' Da says, breaking his worried silence.

'I thought you'd want a chance to see what the adult world was like, and I'm up there thinking you're doing great.'

'I was…' Archie trails off.

'I'm thinking you're in here fermenting the wort, but instead your flipping bloody pancakes,' Da says and disnae realise how funny that is, but Archie flinches as he supresses his smile.

'Well, this distillery has still got to run. Convict or no, you'll see this process through. This might be the only place that will employ you with a criminal record. But let's hope it disnae come to that. Your mother is going to be *disgusted*.'

'I can't say I'm completely sorry, Da. He deserved it. But I should have handled it better,' Archie says, and his face looks fearful. 'Do we need to tell Ma?'

Archie's Da shakes his head in disgust, before storming out. Shit, Archie, now your wee mammy is going to find oot.

With Da gone, Archie's pulled oot his notebook again, trying anything to avoid looking at the blood-spattered floor. The evidence.

'You think you can just bury your head in a book and not face what's just happened?'

It's Alice. Her face is blotchy from crying. She looks in shock. Word has obviously spread by now that Archie has given him a tanking.

'How do u know?' Archie asks defensively, casting the book aside.

'It's all round the distillery, Arch! You've put him in hospital,' she says full of emotion now. 'And it's all my fault! The rest of them have just been shouting at me for it.'

Archie's getting angry again now. Not with Alice, but the other folk treating her bad. He pulls Alice towards him and hugs her.

'C'mere,' he says, inhaling the smell of her strawberry shampoo. 'Naw it's no your fault. It's ma fault! But I couldn't sit and listen to that prick saying he'd been wae ye. Calling you a slag!' Archie rages.

'How did you know he was lying, Arch?' she says, her head is resting on his chest for comfort now.

'I knew you'd wait to be in love Alice. I knew you widnae just go with anyone, and especially not someone like him,' he says, shocked that she would ever think he'd believe Stevie.

I'm beginning to feel a bit awkward guys. I don't know what it is. Maybe it's the way these two are looking at each other. He's turning her chin up, so she'll look at him now.

'And see if you had been with him Alice. I don't care. I'd still do it again. He'd no right to talk about you like that,' he says, as their eyes lock with intensity.

Woooo hoooo! Finally, they're winching! Slow and passionate, and ultimately sickening for us all to watch. She's breaking away and they both look breathless. I'm not surprised, the way they were carrying on.

'I've barely even spoke to the guy Arch, he's a creep!' she says bursting into tears again.

'I just don't understand why he'd say those things. What have I ever done to him?'

'He knows you're out of his league. Believe me if he ever comes near you or so much as mentions your name again, I'll put him back in hospital,' Archie promises, squeezing her slim waist between his hands. Surprise, surprise, they're winching again. They cannae seem to get enough of each other. Then the door to the room swings open and they jump apart instinctively. Caught a belter.

Archie's Da is back again, with replacement staff for the wash house. He flings a coat at Archie.

'Police station,' he commands. Archie smacks the lips on Alice, and you can tell Da isn't happy with it. Even Alice shies away from the look he gees her. The workers smirk at each other and Alice just looks mortified.

'I'll phone you when I'm done,' Archie assures her as he heads for the door.

'Alice, I think you better get back to your post,' Da says gruffly. She scampers by him, averting her eyes. I wish I could go with Arch to the police station, but I'm stuck in here fermenting. Having to listen to these dafties run Archie's name through the mud. Bloody typical.

Chapter 9

Cooperage

Archie:

I can't get it oot of my heid. Ma's tears in the police station. I'm gutted I caused that. I felt like a scumbag, for letting her doon. I can't believe Stevie's pressing charges. He caused the whole thing.

'Are you no concentrating?' Jimmy asks me. We're in the cooperage and I'm learning the process of making barrels.

'Eh, aye Jimmy. Sorry, I was miles away there.'

'You'll no hear anything for months probably son, just put it oot your mind till then,' he counsels kindly. 'He was a prick anyway, any one if us was due to spark him oot soon.'

I'm glad for his kind words. I've been blacklisted around the distillery since. Only a few of the older ones seem to understand, but they probably widnae have been so stupit. Hamish, surprisingly, has had my back over it. He's a good big guy to have on yer side. I don't need to worry about getting jumped by Stevie's wee mates and being made to sleep with the whiskies. I've been blacklisted with my ma and da too. Da's barely even speaking to me and my ma has been too worried sick aboot the police to be chatty. For now, I'm glad to be here, learning a craft and trying to take my mind off it all. Ionach distillery is one of only a handful in Scotland that has its own cooperage on site. Most folk outsource it to someone else, so we're kind of unique here.

'Now normally it takes four years minimum to gain an apprenticeship for Cooperage,' explains Jim, 'but, for some reason your Da just wants us to give you a crash course in the bare bones of it.'

Jim's a barrel-chested man with tattoos completely covering his arms and neck. He's not very talkative but he's got so much professional knowledge.

'How'd you get into this Jimmy?' I ask, watching his fluid like movements in his craft.

'I was always a creative person, but I never really had a direction in life,' he begins to explain, and I know the feeling all too well.

'So, when I left school and was looking for a job, I didnae have scooby what lay in store. I got the chance of the cooper's apprenticeship and snapped it up. Working with wood and my hands seemed like a good option for me.'

I can tell that it was the right decision, from what I've seen today. He's at home amongst the barrels, an artist at work, who wears his leather apron like a second skin. Within the cooperage grounds there are huge stacks of barrels forming whisky pyramids, transported in here by big lorries. I've been told most of a cooper's workload is repairing casks like these. This morning we're working on the cask we're using for my whisky. First Jimmy inspects it for defects.

'We work with mostly American oak and some French and European oak,' he explains as he brushes the barrel to look for imperfections. He's got a wild eye for detail, seeing things I can't identify on it. He makes it seem like a doddle as he continues to chat with me.

'It's always oak we use for casks, Archie, and nothing else,' Jimmy says as he points out the concerning areas and circles them with chalk pulled from his apron.

'This wood is ideal, because the grain is tight. Yer whisky will seep into the wood and back oot without leaking oot the barrel.' Da has told me aw aboot this before, so I'm following it no bother.

'This is an American oak cask we're working with, and all these types of barrels have been used for bourbon before we buy them up and ship them here. The bourbon has already influenced the wood,' he explains.

'Da says we're using first fill for the whisky, what's that all aboot?' I ask, genuinely enjoying learning about it all.

'Aye, that means it's the first time the barrel's been used for whisky. The less the cask has been used, we reckon, leads to more interaction of wood and whisky which can only be a good thing.'

I nod in agreement; my whisky is sounding dynamite already.

'Right, now that we've found all the bits that need work, it's time to repair and replace the staves.' Jimmy sets to work with tools I've never seen before to separate the staves, the strips of wood that combine to make the barrel. Once he's repaired the damage and replaced the staves, he leads me over to the charrer.

'This is the charring machine,' he says as the barrel is sacrificed to it like a wicker man. 'Gas jets help to burn the inside of the cask, which we do for roughly four minutes.' As we monitor the charring he continues to explain the process.

'Charring the inside gives the oak a new lease of life so they can be used again. The wood's got pores, like our skin.

Charring breaks up those pores and lets the whisky into wood to pick up flavours as it matures.'

We take the charred barrel off the machine and transfer to the steamers.

'Steam softens the wood and makes it malleable for finishing,' Jimmy tells me as we wait.

Next Jimmy adds metal hoops, fitting them tightly to hold the cask together for years.

'It's time for the hoop driver,' he says taking me to another machine where the hoops are pressed and made ready for testing. He uses a big hose to pump compressed air into the cask, turning it around to check for leaks.

'Now we'll be adding a rubber bung,' he says placing the bung into the hole in the centre of the cask. 'And since there are no leaks, we can give it the cooperage stamp of approval.' I watch him label the barrel with the stamp and feel buzzing about oor work today. I actually forgot aboot my problems for a while, but I haven't forgot aboot Alice.

'Right, Arch,' he says, proudly patting me on the back. 'I hope ye learned aw ye want to know about cooperage. Cause I'm getting rid of ye noo. I've got work up tae my eyeballs.'

'Aye, that was brilliant the day Jim, thanks so much,' I beam.

'Great son, ye can go away and enjoy the rest of yer day,' he says and I'm off like a shot to meet Alice.

I wait for her to get her break up behind the stables. It's far enough away from the distillery to not be seen, but close enough for her to get back in time. My heart's thundering, waiting on her, and I wipe my sweaty palms on my overalls. The grass is dry behind the stables, as it's been a brilliant day. So, I park myself down, pulling up blades of grass.

Alice has just arrived, and she looks like an angel as the sun sits at her back. I pull her down towards me and we kiss. She's got the softest lips I've ever felt. The grass tickles oor necks.

'I could do that aw day,' I say as she pulls away from me. She doesn't look as happy as me, and she sits up ripping blades from the ground and tossing them aside.

'What's wrong?' I ask her, with my arm now around her waist.

She sighs, before starting on me. She looks raging to be honest, a colour I've no really seen on her yet. But she's still stunning.

'You saw the way your Da looked at me the other day. He's raging about us. I'm his employee, it's a conflict of interest.'

'He probably just knows you've got me wrapped around your finger,' I say kissing her neck and trying to make her forget how angry she seems to be at me. Despite enjoying it, she pulls away, adamant in her annoyance. What chance have I got?

'Your Da always liked me, and now we've messed that all up,' she says, obviously gutted to think he's fell oot wae her. I try and reassure her.

'Look, my Da's a bit of a control freak. So, he probably is a wee bit annoyed with us, that we made a decision for ourselves without consulting him,' I laugh. 'But I think his reaction was more towards the fact I might have got myself a criminal record,' I say trying to explain Da's cold demeanour.

'I'll be telling him just how much you mean to me and how this isnae just some silly fling. But I'll need to wait till he's calmed doon a bit and will actually give me the time of day.'

Something about Alice's silence scares me. Before long she blurts out how she really feels.

'I don't want you to tell him, Archie,' she says, and I feel like I've been battered in the baws.

'If he asks, you can just say it was a one off. A kiss between friends. I still need to work here you know, and I don't want any animosity with my gaffer.'

I cannae believe she wants to dingy this. I want to shout it from the top of the hills, but she wants to play it doon. I don't know what to say without coming off like a wee boy. I've never really had a bird before, and it looks like I still don't.

'I just don't want everyone knowing Arch, I'll get treated differently. I just want to be my own person here,' she justifies, looking guilty. My face has obviously given me away. My ma always say's I'm a rotten liar, as my face tells the whole story.

'I mean my mum and dad don't even know yet, I don't want to make a fool of them.'

I can see that she's really worried about it all, maybe even a little scared. I don't want cold feet to make me lose her, so I'll say anything I can to keep her.

'Let's just take it slow,' I say, pulling her towards me again and this time she doesn't resist. I kiss her lips softly, 'Ye do like me still, Alice?'

'I more than like you, that's the problem. It's just such a big age gap too, Arch,' she says, toying with the back of my hair. I kiss her again, showing her that the age gap means nothing.

'Keep it just us for a wee while longer. Before other people try and ruin it,' she says. How many excuses is she going to come up with?

'I've telt Hamish already,' I confess sheepishly, and instantly I can see her hackles going up. 'But we're good mates now, I'm sure he'll no say anything. I'll tell him to keep quiet, it's sound.'

'He's a fud.'

'What? Naw, that's my big mate.'

'He chatted me up before I'd even spoken a word to him. So, so shallow, Archie and absolutely loves himself,' she says, appalled that I'm keeping such company clearly.

'Well, I'm glad you had good taste and waited for somebody better looking.'

'I mean it, Arch, I don't get good vibes from him. Wasn't he horrible to you when you first started helping out?' she asks, and her angry tone is back.

'He was just bursting ma baws, that's what guys do to each other.'

'You should always trust your first instinct Arch. Don't be unfair to people, but just be aware. You're not often wrong with your first impression.'

'You thought I was too young for you,' I say, grabbing her in for a kiss again. She melts, releasing that gorgeous smile.

'You'll just need to prove me wrong.'

Chapter 10
The Still House
Barley:

It's me again, Barley, and I'm here in the still house. It's the big place where I change from weak wash and put on my big boy whisky pants. Alice is here, failing to ignore Archie as he tries to put her aff her work.

'Look you pest, Jim and your da will be in any minute. I cannae have this, I'm at my work,' she giggles as his hands roam her body.

I've kindly averted my eyes, cause I'm no a perve, but Hoppo says that Archie and Alice are winching. They better watch, or they'll get caught.

Hawl! Archie! I can hear yer da and James coming. They've pulled away from each other and Archie's jumped doon the steps, just before they come to the door. Alice sits at her station at the spirit safe, writing in her notes.

'Ready to get started son?' Da asks, and Archie jumps at the chance to speak to him. I don't think it has been all sunshine with the family since the incident.

'Aye Da, cannae wait,' he says bursting with enthusiasm. Everyone in the room smiles. Yer making yourself look like a total noob, Archie.

'Brilliant,' Da says with a laugh and I think Archie's just glad to be getting acknowledged by him again. 'In the wash house, we fermented the *Wort* to produce a strong beer-type liquid known as *Wash*. Hence the name wash house,' he begins.

I prefer to think of it as the place Archie rinsed that scumbag Stevie oot, but each to their own.

'It's transferred in here via the big copper pipes into this first still, the wash still,' Da says as their eyes follow the pipes to the wash still. We're in a big bell-shaped contraption with a long neck that flows into a condenser. This is the wash still Da's talking aboot.

'We'll charge about 14,600 litres of wash into these stills,' says Da, and I can see Archie taken aback by the amount of liquid about to pass in here.

'The wash still is heated until we boil the liquid.' Jimmy busies himself at his post and soon the room is filled with a constant background noise like air gushing. It's almost like someone is hushing us all. The temperature in the room is rising too. In here we're bloody roasting.

'The vapours, which all have different boiling points, gradually ascend up the still body into the line arm, ye can see, which feeds into the condenser,' Da says and I start to feel like I might take a panic attack. I'm moving oot of my body, leaving the wash behind and floating up to the top of the still as a vapour. We move into the line arm and then into the condenser. The cold air is a shock to oor systems, and we find ourselves transferring back into oor liquid form and moving through the spirit safe that Jimmy and Alice monitor. Archie and Da join them to see us. Hellooooo!

'The vapour has condensed and runs back into this spirit safe,' Da explains 'and we'll collect what we call the low wines from the wash still here. Its roughly twenty-two percent alcohol now. But that's not good enough for whisky yet.'

We're directed into a second big still, feeling so much stronger than we did back in the wash house. Again, they're roasting us alive. Another outer body experience and then we're condensed back to liquid and rattled into the spirit safe.

'In what we call the spirit still, the liquid is boiled up and condensed again,' coaches Archie's Da, and Archie notes it all down in his wee book. 'It increases from twenty-two percent ABV to sixty-four point five.' That explains why we feel brilliant now.

'But instead of just one run into the receiver we have three fractions of the spirit run. This is where the mastery sets in. In the still house it's a perfect science and we want to collect only the middle run of the whisky. We don't want the ends or the start, just the middle bit which is perfect for consumption. Its crucial to have highly skilled people like James and Alice on our team,' says Da, and the pair are visibly honoured by the comment.

'The first fraction is the fore shot, it's all the bad stuff we don't want to drink,' Da explains, as they group around the safe.

'We don't throw this away though cause we can use it in the next distillation,' Archie soaks up all the knowledge and shares a wee smile with Alice.

'The middle run we take is the new make spirit that we want to collect for filling in the warehouse. We do this at 64.5% alcohol on the run and change the dish in the safe at this point.' James changes the dish and we begin to be separated.

I'm being siphoned off, out of the run and transferred along long copper pipes to the vats in the barrel filling warehouse. I've still got wee Hoppo with me, thank god.

'Aye, happy to have me with ye now, ye big shitebag!'

Och, well Hoppo, it's not a case of fear really, it's just nice to have a bit of back up from yer best mate. Even if he is a half-wit. As we travel along the pipes, we can still hear the chat.

'The last part of the run is the feints, and we collect these and run the spirit right the way down to 1.8%, then put the still off,' Da says drawing the process to a close.

'Excellent,' says Archie, 'so, what happens with the stuff that's left over, Da?'

'The by-product that's left over is used to preheat the next distillation run,' Da says, throwing an arm around Archie proudly.

'Well congratulations son!' he cheers. 'You've just distilled your first batch of whisky. This is a day you will remember for the rest of yer life Archie,'

'Aye Da,' Archie beams, 'I'll remember this forever.'

Chapter 11
Acceptance
Barley:

'I got into Dundee uni, Da,' Archie confesses as he and Da roll through the barrel he helped char and repair in the cooperage. Da looks like he could rocket through the roof with pride. His chest swells and he grabs him into a bear hug, crunching him dearly.

'Absolutely brilliant pal!' he says, slapping him on the back with his huge hand. Da's form of affection looks painful.

'I still don't know whether to go,' Archie says, 'I feel like I'm waiting for the guillotine to drop, waiting on this verdict.'

'You're going,' Da says firmly. 'We made a deal remember. I'm no having you back here till you've done it. Because let me tell you, that missed opportunity will haunt you for the rest of your life.'

Archie's Da uses a big flat head screwdriver type-tool to remove the barrel's rubber bung. There is a piece of burlap over the hole, which he places to the side. He reaches over to the machine that links to oor vat and hands Archie a big hose. Archie places it into the bunghole and they turn on the machine. The noise starts up as the hose pipes us from the new make spirit vat into the barrel. Here, wait a minute! It's a bit claustrophobic in here, Archie.

'Go and try it. Give it a year. If you don't like it at least you've got the modules for a year. You might love it,' says Da as they fill the barrel and some of oor new make spirit sloshes out. They quickly cut aff the machine to avoid waste.

'The police thing could take another year to come through, don't put your life on hold for that,' Da advises, pulling a fresh rubber bung from sterilising fluid.

'We'll deal wae that as a family when the time comes,' he says as he hands Archie the bung and he places it in the bunghole.

'Hammer it in gently with the mallet, son.' Archie quietly contemplates, as they roll oor barrel onto a pallet ready to be taken to the cold maturation warehouse.

'So, that's you just filled a first-fill whisky cask. That's another string to yer bow son,' Da says nudging him. Archie still looks miles away.

'What's going on wae ye?' asks Da.

'I'm worried about being away from Alice,' Archie says dejectedly, forgetting his promise to keep it all a secret.

'Don't put off your future for something that might just be a flash in the pan,' Da says, looking slightly annoyed. Meanwhile Archie's clearly offended. Does Da not know how much he likes Alice?

'I'm no trying to patronise you son, but it's the first lassie you've ever had a sniff of. There's a whole world of them oot there and you've got all your life to find the right person. Do you really think you've found her at 17? How likely is that?'

'I'm 18 shortly,' he justifies, but Da's already off on another lecture.

'Look she's a beautiful lassie, and a lovely person too Arch, but you've got bother wae the polis now,' he snaps, making his feelings clear. Alice is leading his boy astray.

'It's not Alice's fault I attacked him!'

'Don't gees it. When men do something stupit ye can always bet there's a wummin involved. We cannae help but perform for them,' Da says shooting doon his argument.

He points a finger at Archie's chest, 'If you weren't wrapped up in her it would never have happened. And you know that.'

Poor Archie, he can't find an answer for it. Of course, he disnae blame Alice, but he's never cared so much about anyone, so the thought of anyone hurting her sends him wild. He's no rational about her.

'Look she's older too Archie. Won't be long before someone her own age turns her head. Someone who can take her places.'

Archie looks gutted. Kick a man while he's doon why don't ye?

'She has said I'm maybe a bit too young, cause I've no even been into the pubs yet,' confesses Archie, walking away to the door and looking out at the distillery grounds. He looks so sad, like he knows he's not got a real chance.

It seems like maybe Archie's Da has softened a wee bit. He obviously sees how gutted he is. Ye need to just trust that yer weans can make their own decisions and be there when it all goes up in smoke, I think.

'I'll get ye intae the pub, nae bother. And I'll be the one to show you how to drink. With a temper like yours, I'm no having you not knowing how to drink properly. God knows what ye'd get up tae,' says Da, putting an arm around him at the doorway. Archie's face lights up.

'You'll start coming for a pint with your auld Da, tomorrow in fact,' he chuckles. 'Yer ma will no be happy, but I'll swing it for ye.'

'Cheers, Da.'

'I know you're going to do what you need to do, Archie. I know you'll no listen tae me. Why start now? But just try not to fall head over heels.'

Think it's too late for that one, oor Archie is already smitten.

'If she isnae happy for ye when you tell her about Dundee, that will be the test. She cannae be the one for ye, if she's no happy. She should want the best for you.'

They both head out of the building and before they part ways, Archie's da says 'Look, you've got your driving test next week. Smash it and then that will be another thing to show her. You can be the one to take her places.' Archie laughs and they part ways. Da goes back up to his office and Archie sneaks away to the maturation warehouse where he's meeting Alice.

The forklift driver delivers me there, and I wait to be racked up another day. It's a cold warehouse with hundreds of other barrels in front of me. On the walls there is funny white stuff that looks like fungus. Looks a bit clatty to me.

'That's just the fungus that occurs when the Angel's take their share,' pipes up Hoppo. Angel's share?

'Yeah! Every year that whisky matures in here, a small amount of the alcohol evaporates. People like to think the angels come and take a wee drink. But really when it evaporates it condenses on the ceiling and walls and causes moisture. And then the white stuff thrives.'

Well look at professor Hoppo. A real fun-gi!

Archie has his own keys to the place now, and he waits around for Alice. He reads his official acceptance letter again. Chap, Chap, Chap! He pushes the letter into his pocket. He opens the door to Alice who's wrapping herself around him nearly knocking him off his feet. They back into the room, still kissing.

'I passed my assessment the other day, we should go celebrate tomorrow!' squeals Alice in excitement.

'Oh, I've got to go for a pint with my Da tomorrow,' he apologises, and he pushes the acceptance letter deeper into his pocket.

Alice looks shocked, it's not like Archie to pass up on time with her. But I'm sure she knows a boy needs time with his da.

'That's nice you're going to spend a bit of time together,' she says, trying to hide her disappointment.

'I need to try, we're just getting back to being pals again,' he justifies, seeing her disappointment.

'Oh definitely, we can rain check for another day,' she says more convincingly this time. They kiss each other deeply. It comes time for them to leave and Archie leaves first to avoid suspicions. He hands Alice a key, before he goes.

'What? I'll get my books for having this, Archie.'

'Look, it's a copy, Da will never know,' he says, 'I trust ye, so just don't get caught.'

Archie sneaks off and Alice hangs back to avoid being seen with him. She looks at the array of whisky in front of her. It amazes her. She disnae realise someone is also watching her.

'Alright Alice,' he says with a big sleazy grin.

'Hello Hamish,' Alice says, her shoulders have aw tightened up. You can tell she disnae like the guy. I'm with her on that, he's a Grade-A creep. I can't believe Archie hangs aboot wae him now.

'Just heard Archie knocking ye back for celebrating,' says Hamish nosily.

'He's already got plans with his da, it's no big deal,' she says, a bit too defensively.

'Ye can come wae us,' Hamish offers, seedily. 'I'm going doon to see this barmaid all the boys are talking aboot.'

You've perked her interest with that Hamish.

'Good looking, is she?' Alice asks, trying to seem aloof.

'I've not seen her yet, but the boys say she's stunning. Some arse on her Archie says,' Hamish purrs with a cunning smile.

No way did Archie say that, he's a gentleman. I'm not saying he doesn't appreciate a nice bum, but I know he's only got eyes for Alice.

'Did he say that?' Alice asks raging, cheeks flaring up. The creep's coming closer to her. He flicks the ponytail off her shoulder and that makes her shiver.

'She's probably no a patch on you don't worry,' he says. 'Don't sit in by yourself come doon with all of us.'

'I'll pass thanks,' she says coldly.

'Suit yerself, let me know if ye change yer mind,' says Hamish, looking rather pleased with himself as he slinks oot of the warehouse.

Chapter 12
Maturation
Barley:

I've been racked up here in the warehouse, where I've been busy maturing. Really, it's just a lot of sitting about in this barrel. I can already feel subtle changes in myself, but I've a long way to go until I'm technically malt whisky. But see when I am, I'll be special. Just you wait. Since I've been here its become tradition that this is where the love birds come to meet. It's usually deserted and private enough for them to get a wee winch and catch up on each other's day. Here they are together again.

'I got my grades through and I've been accepted to Dundee, Alice,' he says sheepishly. It's taken him ages to work up to this. He's trying to gauge her reaction. Alice kisses him deeply and he looks relieved. She's happy for ye Archie, that's brilliant mate!

'That's fab, I'm so proud of you,' Alice says with sadness tinging her voice. He brings the letter oot of his overalls, and she inspects it. It's true Alice. I think she notices the date on the letter, as her forehead wrinkles, but she chooses not to say anything.

'You'll need to come back home and visit me Arch, you know I can't drive,' she says, sounding almost panicky. 'If you still want to that is.'

'Course I do, just try and keep me away,' he says, hugging her tight.

'You're going to have all your uni work, and you'll be having a blast doing all the fresher's stuff. You'll not be wanting to come back to see me.'

'Don't be daft, I cannae live without you ya spoon!' says Archie shocked by her suggestions. They kiss again for a while, but Alice is like a dug wae a bone and wants to talk aboot it more.

'I don't want to hold you back, if you're moving on with your life,' she says pulling him back to reality.

'I'm still going to be the same person Alice, just with a degree,' he assures her and squeezes her hand.

'So, I don't need to worry? You won't forget all about me then?'

'Never, Alice,' he says. 'You're scarred into my brain.'

'Charming!' she says laughing.

'It's a compliment, believe me. Look, I even wrote something for you,' Archie says fishing oot another crumpled sheet of paper.

'It's a sonnet. It was bloody hard to do, but there's a module I'll be doing on creative writing, so I thought I'd give myself a head start.'

Alice reads and when tears start to form in her eyes, she buries her head into Archie's chest, mumbling, 'What are you doing to me?'

When she has composed herself, she says wistfully, 'I wish I could be as creative as that.'

Archie raises an eyebrow.

'What about all those sketches I see scattered all around the cottage? You're talented too Alice.'

'Yeah, but your talent is actually useful. I mean you're so talented, you should be writing any chance you get and trying to get published.'

'I couldnae write a book. Think how much work goes into it. I never finish anything,'

Archie says, dismissing the idea instantly.

'You'll have a best seller by the end of your course with all that stuff you're going to learn.'

Alice kisses him again and before they know it they are sinking to the floor and cuddling in the isle between the racks.

'I want to tell everyone about us, Alice. I'm sick of keeping this feeling to myself.'

'Ok,' she agrees, and Archie is thrilled. She must see a future if she's willing to come clean to everyone. 'I need you to meet my mum and dad first, I can't have them being the last to know.'

'Aye nae bother, I'd love to meet them,' says Archie excitedly. 'When can we do it?'

'I'm going back home in two weeks, come with me?' she asks hopefully.

'I'll drive us babe, that's the handy thing about having a boyfriend with a license now,' he agrees readily, making sure to boast.

'That would be amazing, would your Dad let you have the car?'

'I don't see why not.'

'Great! We can stay the weekend and I'll show you about Luss and let you get to know them,' she says snuggling into him.

'Sounds like a plan.'

Meeting the parents? That's a big deal Archie. I can tell by the look on his face he's already beginning to brick it.

Chapter 13
Love
Barley:

Archie's come into my warehouse, practically dragging Alice by the wrist. Trouble in paradise it seems. I miss all the drama cooped up in here honestly. Last I saw these two, they were away to Luss to meet the parents. Maybe it didnae go well. Let's have a listen and see what the goss is.

'Piss off Archie!' she says pulling herself away.

'Naw. Come and speak to me. You've not spoken to me since we got back and you can barely even look at me,' Archie says, and his voice is full of confusion.

'When would I have a chance to speak to you? When your propping up the bar talking to that slag?' Alice spits the accusation at him.

'Hey, wait a minute, I told you I was going for a pint with Hamish when I came back. And she's no a slag, that's pish! She's a nice lassie.'

'Aye very good Archie,' she says, rolling her eyes and folding her arms against her chest.

'What's with the attitude?'

'First chance you get, you patch me for you pals,' she says, 'couldn't wait to get out of my company obviously.'

'Look I'd just sat and took all the pish of the day off your family! I needed to blow off steam,' Archie bursts oot, he looks raging now. What did they say to ye big man?

'I know they're not the easiest, but they're my family and you had to meet them,' she says defensively, yet a guilty look appears on her face. I can tell they've been shite to him, obviously. Why else is all hell breaking loose between these two?

'Well, there was basically no point. They were never going to give their approval,' he snaps back.

'Well, you never really made an effort in my opinion. You would think since you claim to have all these feelings for me you'd have tried to impress them a little,' Alice goads, and Archie narrows his eyes in response.

'Impress them?' he says coolly, 'I'm not a performing monkey. If they cannae see what I'm all about, then screw them.'

'Screw them?' Alice is absolutely raging now. 'That's my mum and Dad you're talking about, just remember that blood is thicker than water.'

'I was a write off to them as soon as I walked in the door.'

'Bullshit Archie.'

'Och, just try and deny it! The wee comments and putdowns as subtle as a brick. It was a lovely visit, aye!' Archie says sarcastically.

'So what?' retorts Alice with contempt. 'They're my parents, you're supposed to play ball and prove yourself to them. Try and create a good impression for goodness sake.'

'I shouldn't need to do that,' Archie shakes his head in disbelief.

'And why not? Are they supposed to just blindly trust you with their Daughter?'

'It should be up to you Alice, you've picked me, it's your judgement that counts.'

'Well, I'm beginning to doubt my judgement on your maturity. Any one *my* age would have known how to act,' she says, delivering the stinging remark.

'I'm sorry I didn't realise it was an interview that mattered,' Archie replies, giving off the impression he isn't bothered in the slightest.

'Of course it does Archie! I'm a girl. I'm close to my parents and their opinion will always matter.'

Uh-Oh! This boy can argue till he's blue in the face, but Archie is panicking now. The big man knows that he's pushed it too far. Archie, from the sounds of it they gave you a hard time. But it's the lassie's parents ya numpty. You need to take the hazing until your initiated into the family. It's like an unwritten rule. People get protective over their wee lassies.

'Look,' Archie says pulling her in tight around the waist, 'I'm sorry. I've never met anyone's parents before. I just got offended when your Da was slagging my degree off, and when your maw criticised my family's business. I felt they didn't like me, so I put up the barriers.'

'I'm sorry my Dad wound you up about the degree Archie, he's just one of these old school practical guys,' said Alice sincerely, 'And mum hates all alcohol. She's a bit of a prude yeah, but she has her reasons. She can't keep her opinions to herself and believe me I hate it too.' She pushes Archie further away, distancing herself, and placing her hand on his chest. She says seriously, 'But she has a heart of gold, so to judge her based on one night wouldn't be fair to me.'

'I know, I know,' he says pulling her in again and this time she allows her head to lie on his chest in their hug.

'Does that mean you hate me now?' asks Archie.

'No!' Alice says in frustration, pulling him down to her for a kiss, with a hand entangled in his t-shirt.

'I love you,' she whispers, voice shaking. She looks like she wishes she could take the words back instantly. I don't think they've ever told each other before.

'I love you too Alice,' Archie says, smacking the lips on her again. 'I'm no gaunae let you doon like that again.'

'And you think you can put up with my mad family?' Alice laughs, covering her mouth. Archie stops her hand and kisses the inside of her palm.

'Anything for you,' Arches says, grabbing her bum. 'Especially with a bum like that!'

Alice laughs and throws herself into another kiss.

They two are always winching, but there's something different this time. Maybe it's because they love each other now. Maybe I shouldn't be watching this. Their hands are all over each other and they seem almost frantic.

'Did your mum never tell you about the birds and the bees Barley?'

Eh? The birds and the bees deliver wee baby grains to the field?'

'Aye something like that!'

Alice pulls away, lips and cheeks flushed.

'You alright?' Archie says pulling her back against him.

'Yeah,' she says breathing deeply. 'I just want to make sure if we do this…'

'This?' says Archie kissing down her neck and making her squirm.

'*This,*' Alice says, forcing him to take her seriously. 'If we do this Arch, then it has to be forever, you do know that don't you? This means something, and I don't want to go there without a future.'

'I don't want to ever be without you,' Archie says stroking her hair, 'I don't even care if it sounds cheesy

Alice, I'd marry you in a heartbeat. The boys call you Super-Alice because I just cannae see by you.'

'Forever then?' Alice says melting into deep kiss with Archie again.

'Forever.' Archie says, before they pounce on each.

Quick Hoppo, turn around! This is definitely not for us to see, ye wee pervert. We shouldn't be allowed to see this for at least another eighteen years.

Chapter 14
1-7-3
Barley:

I've been here for months maturing in the cask. The oak is apparently changing and developing our flavour. I've overheard them saying that I cannae go about saying I'm whisky yet. I need to wait in here for 3 years minimum. Even then, there's no way Archie or his Da's going to bottle us there and then. Nobody wants a minimum aged whisky apparently. So, I'll be stuck in here till god knows when. It's a bit like a prison sentence. But at least my big mate Archie still comes to visit me. Even if it is under the pretence of getting some nookie off the lovely Alice. Course we always allow them privacy. They're lying on their wee blanket the now wrapped up in each other's arms. They must be bloody baltic.

'I could do that aw day, every day, until we just wasted away from not feeding ourselves,' says Archie still planting kisses all over Alice's shoulders. She gives a great belly laugh now, but she doesn't hide her mouth anymore. Archie's eventually made her love her smile.

'You're aff yer heid do you know that?' she says pinning him down and returning his kiss.

'You think that, but you don't know how beautiful you look right now,' Archie says, and he looks like he's looking at an angel. Alice can do no wrong in his eyes.

'Well we better hurry and get dressed before my break is done and someone walks in and *sees* how beautiful I am,' she laughs again, scampering around the isle between the stacks for her clothes and dressing with stealth.

Archie watches her for a while, lounging on the blanket propped on one arm.

'Move it Archie, your Da will be looking for you,' she says prodding him with her toe, before slipping her feet back into her boots.

'Shit, aye!' he says launching to his feet, as if waking up finally. 'I've to take my ma for her check-up, Da's got the accountant coming.'

When the pair are dressed Alice packs away their wee blanket into her backpack and combs her long brown hair back into a ponytail.

'Gorgeous,' Archie says, pulling her in for a cuddle.

'I think I'll fancy you forever you know,' he says, 'I can't get you oot ma mind.'

'Ah but will you still fancy me when I'm all grey and I've lost my looks?' asks Alice, snuggling under his arm.

'Och aye, I'll always fancy you. Even when you're old,' he winks.

'You'll be old too,' Alice reminds him.

'Aye but I'll age well!' he smirks. 'Plus, I'll still be younger.'

'Cheeky sod,' she says squeezing him tight. 'Nice to know your love's not shallow.'

'Course, I love you hunners,' he assures her.

'I love you millions, Archie,' Alice says.

'I love you 1-7-3!' Archie says and they both erupt in laughter.

'Now I know how much I mean to you,' Alice says batting him on the stomach.

'Naw, listen that's a good number. Let me tell you. It means I'll love you for one whole lifetime. I'll love you for the seven babies you're going to give me—' Archie starts to explain.

'You can fuck right off, there will not be seven babies!' she says, gutting herself laughing.

'Let me finish… and I love you for 3 reasons. You're the kindest person I know, you're the best friend I've ever had and your bum,' Archie says patting her bum, 'is the out of this world.'

'Och Archie, that's actually very romantic,' Alice says, touched.

'That's me, you just never know when I'm going to surprise you,' he says. 'Ladies first, we don't want to raise any suspicions.'

'Ok babe. Come round tonight when you're done, I'll cook us dinner,' Alice delivers him one final peck before slipping oot of warehouse. Archie flicks through his phone, perched on a nearby stool killing time. It rings in his hand, and he answers.

'Nothing much mate, how?' I hear him say.

'Aye sound mate, I'll meet you for a drink after I take my ma for her appointment,' he says as he leaves. The phone is glued to his ear and he's laughing at whoever is on the other end.

Aw well Hoppo, guess he's forgotten all aboot Alice's dinner.

Chapter 15
The Bug
Barley:

Alice looks awful. I mean, really peely-wally. I've just seen her dry wretch. Maybe she's caught a wee bug or something. Her eyes are all puffy though, seems like she might have been crying. She's waiting for Archie doon here. In he stoats, looking guilty. Her eyes are burning right through him.

'I'm sorry I missed dinner,' he says rubbing the back of his neck.

'Could you not even have answered your phone?' Alice says, eyes blazing.

'Eh, I ran out of battery, I'm sorry,' he says approaching her cautiously. 'I'll make it up to you tonight, I'll get us a takeaway or something.'

'Where were you?' she asks, arms folded defensively. She looks like she's struggling not to be sick now.

'I went down to meet Hamish for a quick pint and then time just got away from me. I didn't intend that, I'm sorry, Alice. I fucked up.'

Alice looks exhausted and exhales, looking at the ceiling now.

'Are you ok?' Archie says, concerned. 'You look unwell.'

Alice wraps her arms around herself.

'No, I'm feeling horrible. I was sick last night,' she says, looking worried.

'You've maybe got a wee bug,' Archie says, pulling her into a cuddle.

Alice rests her head on his chest, eyes watering again. She wipes away a wee tear that drops from her eye before pushing Archie away.

'You better stay away in case you catch it,' she says coldly, sniffing.

'Do you not want me to come and look after you tonight?' Archie says trying to win her over.

'Thanks, but I think I just need an early night,' Alice says, forcing a sad smile.

'See you later, Arch,' she says kissing him on the cheek and leaving.

'Shit!' Archie says to himself.

Aye, ye made an arse of that one mate.

Chapter 16
The Pub
Archie:

We're in the pub, me and Hamish, perched at our usual spot at the bar. It's half eleven and we've been here since about six. So, you can guess that we're a wee bit worse for wear. We've been talking about Alice and how she was with me today. I know I shouldn't involve Hamish, cause she despises him, but I need someone to talk to.

'Sounds like she's getting a wee bit full on. A wee bit possessive eh?' says Hamish, taking a long slurp of his pint.

'Nah!' I say, straight to Alice's defence. 'She really isn't like that; I think I've just pissed her off for patching her again.'

'Aye they're aw on their best behaviour in the beginning,' he says wiping the foam from his lips, 'Its aw – "I wake up looking like this" and "it's up to you honey, you can pick" –
and before you know it your waking up to Fiona from Shrek and she's controlling your every move.'

I laugh at him, shaking my head.

'That's just the birds you attract I think mate.'

'Come on, Archie,' he says seriously, 'you cannae even get oot for a pint.'

Before I can say any more, he's attracted Louise's attention for another round.

'What you having boys?' she smiles, leaning over the bar with her eyes fixed on me.

'Same again, darling,' says Hamish, but her eyes are still fixed on me and a good job too or she'd see Hamish ogling her cleavage.

'No problem honey,' she says giving him a quick glance and me an even bigger smile.

'How'd you no just be single like me?' asks Hamish, as she busies herself pulling oor pints.

'Because I love Alice,' I say simply. There isn't any other option for me. She's the one.

'So? You think that's going to last forever? Sooner or later you're going to do each other's nut in and you'll be off to find other people.'

'I can't see it, mate,' I say trying to hide my annoyance at the thought of Alice with someone else. I'd have to find the guy and mash his face in so she could never kiss him again. Stevie's bloody face invades my mind. I shiver and drown it out with the dregs of my glass. I'm still waiting on the police getting back to me.

'She's already getting pissed off with ye. I cannae imagine a good-looking lassie like that will be waiting around for ye while you stoat about uni,' Hamish says as Louise returns placing the pints carefully on the beermats in front of us. I can't help but look at the cleavage as she does, but quickly advert my eyes. I feel bad.

'Put it on my tab please,' says Hamish with a wink and she disappears to the other end of the bar to serve other customers.

'Mon oot for a puff,' says Hamish elbowing me as he picks his cigarette packet oot of his pocket. We make our way through the maze of tables to the entrance and camp there while Hamish has his cigarette.

'You want one?' he says offering the carton.

'Nah, they're stinking mate. Don't know how you can manage it,' I say taking a swig of my pint. We move to let one of the auld boys into the pub and he gives us a gracious nod.

'How you doin' boys,' he chuckles, barrelling in for his wee night cap.

'Look, the Alice thing, all I'm saying is… well, maybe it would be better for both of ye if you just ended it now,' Hamish counsels, taking long draws of his cigarette and puffing the smoke away from me.

'You'd have more fun being single. You could take wee Louise out for a drink and have a bit of fun,' he says raising his eyebrows.

'Louise? Naw! She's a lovely lassie, but I'm sure she's no interested,'

'She's practically got her tits in yer pint mate! I think you need to wake up a wee bit,' he laughs, putting out his cigarette and swooping an arm round me as we go back in.

'That's my point,' he says leaning into my ear to talk, 'you've been with Alice too young. You've not even given yerself a chance. Ye don't even know when someone fancies ye.'

We take our seats again and Louise approaches, starting to get a wee head start on settling up for the night. She chats away to us as she cleans behind the bar.

'Hard Day at the office?' she asks, smiling at me. 'Don't think I've seen you look this glum.'

'My heads mangled,' I say, 'just one of those days, Louise.'

She rolls up the sleeve of her shirt, and shows me a freshly inked tattoo, on the inside of her forearm. It's a huge lotus flower, and the start of a sleeve by the looks of it.

'You think your day was bad,' she winces showing off the colourful design. The skin surrounding looks sore and red. 'The swelling will be down by tomorrow.'

'Was it agony?' I say, sucking in air and imagining the needle pricking my own skin.

'Nah, not really. It's a funny sort of pain, sort of addictive,' she explains. 'You ask anyone with a tatoo, they'll tell ye the same thing.'

She flips the back of her dark curls up and ties her hair into a loose bun. She shows me the inking on the back of her neck 'Louise' it reads in fancy calligraphy.

'I got that when I was 16, and I hate it. But the rest of my tattoos I love,' she explains.

Hamish comes back from the toilet and starts pattering her up. Louise is game for him though; she's got great patter.

~

Another hour passes, with us just having a laugh with Louise. She's gutting herself at my jokes, much to Hamish's dismay. My phone is buzzing in my jacket. I pull it out to check and see a few missed calls from Da. I must not have heard it earlier because the speakers where on. It's on silent. I quickly answer, wondering what shit I'm in for now.

'Archie, can you no answer you bloody phone?' Da shouts at me.

'Sorry Da, it's been on silent, what's up?' I say, cringing to think that my mates can hear him giving me a hard time. So embarrassing some times.

'It's yer Ma,' he says, and my stomach sinks as though I've just jumped off of a building. 'We've had to get her an ambulance into hospital. They're taking her in for an operation,' he says and I feel like I'm going to pass out.

'What?' I ask in disbelief.

'They think her appendix has burst.'

I can't think straight; I can't get any words out.

Both Hamish and Louise have noticed now. They're listening to my every word. I must not have said anything for ages as Da starts shouting at me down the phone again.

'Archie! Are you there? Did ye hear me? Yer ma's in hospital—'

I snap from my catatonic state.

'Da, I'll be there quick. Where is it?'

'Vale of Leven Hospital, just jump in the car and get here as soon as possible.'

'Right,' I say instinctively, and Da's already off the phone. I start grabbing my keys and stuffing them into my pockets.

'Whit's going on?' asks Hamish alarmed. 'I've just bought you another pint.'

'It's my ma, she's been taken in for an emergency operation,' I say, now on autopilot, pulling on my jacket.

'I need to get to Vale of Leven pronto,' I say, ready to boost for the door.

'Wait a minute Archie,' Hamish says panicking. 'How ye gaunae get there? Ye cannae drive, you're pished!'

There's that familiar sinking feeling again. He was right. I was pished and the hospital was miles away. What a fuck up I am, I can't even get to my ma when she needs me.

'I'll call ye a cab. Just sit doon and I'll phone one,' Hamish says trying to calm me doon.

'You'll no get a cab the now,' says Dave, the manager, overhearing all our drama. He turns to Louise, who looks twisted with desire to help.

'Could you no take Archie? I'd let you away now and still pay ye?' Dave offers.

'Aye definitely,' says Louise, grabbing her own keys and phone from the hiding place beneath the bar. 'As long as you'll be ok shutting up yourself.'

'Aye, are you sure Dave?' I say, taken aback by his kindness.

'Look, I'm a big hairy arsed guy and its deed in here the night! I've called last orders anyway. I'll be fine Archie. Tell my big mate Arthur I'm thinking of him,' Dave says with assuring smile.

Louise has her denim jacket on and puts her hand in mine, pulling me out of the pub and towards her wee car. I don't even think about it; my mind is swimming so much with thoughts of Ma that her warm palm in mine is just a comfort. Her hand slips away as she beeps open the car.

'Are you ok, Archie?' she says, genuine concern flooding her dark eyes.

'No, not really. I'm shitting myself,' I confess as we climb in the car.

'She'll be ok, these doctors know what they're doing,' she says kindly, grabbing my hand and squeezing it again. We pull out of the carpark and travel against the dark through the small village. I live outside of the village up on oor distillery grounds, but I'm down here often for the pub and the supermarket of course. It's picturesque. It's the image of Scotland people imagine, especially with the rain bucketing down. Despite the weather, it won't take us long to get to the hospital. It's nearly midnight and the wooded roads are a blur as we speed through the dark and rain. The overhead lighting acts like our guardian angel through the night, with our full beams on whenever it is safe.

We reach the hospital, and sandwich into a space near the entrance. An eerie mist surrounds the place, giving it an ethereal glow. The engine rumbles to a stop. I burst into tears. It's humiliating. A grown man greeting over his ma. I can't even remember the last proper conversation I had with her. I wipe away the tears, ashamed, too scared to look up at Louise. I've made a tit of myself. I don't need to look. Her arms are locked around me, holding me towards her. All I can smell is her silky perfume and the coconut conditioner of her wild curls that surround me. Her lips are on mine now. Her tongue is snaking into my mouth as our bodies press together. And I'm kissing her back.

What the fuck am I doing? After way too long, I pull away from the kiss. She's smiling at me, but all I feel is regret. What the fuck? I think of Alice, and I want to vomit.

'Everything will be ok Arch, you'll see,' Louise says, grabbing my hand again. 'We'll find out where we need to go, and you can wait with your Da.'

She plants a soft kiss on my cheek, inches from my mouth and I'm reminded of my actions.

I leave the car and expect to go alone.

'I'm coming with you! I'm not ditching you till I know you're with your family,' she demands as she follows me. I feel like I'm betraying Alice allowing this, but I just need to get to my ma. We head towards the ghostly building. I'm zombie-like as she takes control. She directs us to the right ward and speaks to reception for me. I feel deaf as her words blur into background noise. I'm not sure if it's shock of what just happened or just the alcohol taking over my system. We find our way down the white, sterile corridors to the waiting area. Two familiar faces wait for me. Da looks pale, tired and fearful. Alice looks shocked. Shocked to see Louise squeeze my shoulders and then disappear away to get me a coffee.

'You're Da phoned when he couldn't get a hold of you, I came as fast as I could,' Alice said in a breathy voice, like the wind had just been knocked out of her.

'It's alright, I gave Archie a lift,' says Louise, perkily, returning with crappy plastic cups of coffee for me and Da.

'I see that,' says Alice, trying not to be impolite, but she's hiding fathoms of rage and hurt beneath her small smile. What have I done? Does she know? Don't be silly, how could she? I try to act casual.

'Oh, I'm sorry love,' says Louise genuinely, 'would you like a coffee too? It's no bother.'

'No thank you, but that's very kind,' she says with a nod. Her eyes burn circles into my soul.

Chapter 17
A Real Man
Alice:

I push Hamish away as he slides his hand down onto my bum.

'What the fuck Hamish, how can you do that to Archie?' I say putting as much distance between me and him as possible.

'His mum's in hospital and you're coming onto his girlfriend,' I say full of confident venom, but underneath, his closeness makes me uncomfortable. There's something about Hamish that scares me; that always has. He eyes me like a predator, and I hate to think of the terrible places his mind goes. Why did I let him into the cottage?

'Archie's no bothered about his ma, or you, he's too busy winching Louise,' he says picking my sketch books from the shelf and examining them. I don't want him all over my things.

'Your full of shit Hamish!' I explode. 'I let you in, out of courtesy to Archie. But you're not my friend and I don't need to sit and listen to ye,' I say pushing past him and opening the door as an invitation to leave.

He closes it shut, leaving his bicep on display as his hand bars the door.

'You might want to consider me as a friend,' he says placing a hand on my waist, which I instantly step away from.

'Archie wants to just carry on with you like nothing happened,' Hamish says moving his body, his back now presses against the door. I'm trapped in my own house.

'But ye know I've always liked you Alice, I don't want to see ye treated like a mug.' The softness of his voice does nothing to make me trust him. He'd say anything to get under my skin.

'Look, I know Archie wouldn't do that to me. There's no way Hamish,' I defend Archie, and I believe my words. He would never hurt me.

'He's been at it for months,' says Hamish, following me again, 'you think I'm the only one he's meeting down the pub?'

Everything he says itches at my subconscious. I hated Archie going down there. I heard the rumours that she fancied him. But I couldn't tell him where to go on a night out, who to speak to. That would be creepy and controlling. Ultimately, I trust him, so I always push these feelings to the back of my mind. Hamish takes my hand and rubs it tenderly, and I feel repulsed by this invasion. I pull my hand free.

'Hamish, you've been trying to get into my knickers from the first day we met, you're not a reliable source,' I say firmly.

'I know you knocked me back Alice. And I'm sorry for being too full on in the beginning. But this is genuine. You deserve a man and not a wee boy that cheats on ye,' he says retreating finally. He leaves the door free to pull on his coat.

'But you must have sensed it yourself,' he says, his words carving chunks out of my heart. 'At the hospital that night, he told me he kissed Louise. When they arrived together you knew something was going on. You can't deny that to yourself.'

Hamish makes his way back to the door and pulls it open, stopping to fuel the fire once more.

'You were there for him when he needed you and he had his lips all over another woman. It's pathetic. I've heard it from her first-hand.'

I meet his accusations with silence, as I don't know what to say. I *was* suspicious that night.

'Ask your precious Archie if he kissed her that night,' says Hamish stepping outside now. 'I bet he won't even give you the respect of honesty.'

I feel drained and unsteady. Surely Archie hasn't done this.

'That's the difference between a man and a wee boy. Men can stand up and admit when they've done wrong,' Hamish says as he closes the door, leaving me reeling. Yet it's not just his words that make me feel this way. I'm also lightheaded. I sit down for a moment, pushing away the nausea.

Before I know what I'm doing, I've got my boots on and I'm heading on foot towards the village. People stop on my way to chat, but I just tell them I'm running late. I see the pub and wait anxiously outside the entrance. I'm arguing with myself now. A text message comes from Archie:

Love you babe, coming home to get some stuff, can I meet you? Xxx

Should I turn back? Why trust a word that slime ball, Hamish, says? But then again, he heard it from the horse's mouth. Why let Louise go about saying that about Archie? I head through the door scanning the pub for her. She pauses at a table with her antibacterial spray and cloth. She knows why I'm here. Her face falls. She's got all the answers I need.

Chapter 18

Confrontation

Barley:

It's Barley here again. I'm just sitting in this oak barrel day after day, waiting for my life to begin. At least oor Alice is here today to keep me company. It's been a while. She's been pacing up and doon the whole time, but now she's running outside. I can hear her being sick, poor soul. That bug's lasting a wee while, I'm starting to get worried about her. With Archie's ma in the hospital still, that's aw we need. Enid's appendix burst and when they went in to remove it, they found all sorts of tumours. Most got removed with the appendix, but she'll need treatment for the stuff that spread. Arch has been in bits about it; we all have. He even comes doon here alone sometimes to get away from it all. He writes in his book and greets. Well I'd be greeting too if my mammy was ill. I want to greet even thinking about her. I miss her so much. My da too, and the field. Anyway, we just cannae have Alice falling ill too.

She's back in, pacing up and down again. You'll wear a hole in the floor wummin! Archie arrives and instinctively tries to pull her in for a cuddle. Alice resists, pushing a palm against his chest to keep him away.

'What's going on?' he asks, clearly irritated. 'I've came away from my ma to come see you and you're acting like this.'

'Why was that Louise with you at the hospital?' Alice asks stonily.

Archie looks uneasy, guilty even. Whits this aw aboot Hoppo?

'Look, I was at the pub and I couldn't drive because I was half pished. Dave let her away to help me and ma da out. Simple as that. You don't need to read any more into it,' he says running his hand through his hair.

There is a long, cold silence as Alice eyeballs him. What in the name of the wee man have you done, Archie?

'Did you kiss her?' Alice asks, with her eyes looking fearful now. No way Alice, you've got the wrong end of the stick, pal. Not Archie. He practically worships ye.

'What?' Archie scoffs, offended. 'Do you really think I'd do that to you?'

'Did you *KISS* her?' Alice presses getting angrier by the minute.

Archie looks panicked now, but keeps up his exasperated front.

'My ma's in hospital and your accusing me. You're fucking aff yer heid!' he snaps, trying to storm oot of the warehouse.

Alice grabs him by his jumper, pulling him so hard she's stretched it all out of shape.

'Answer the question Archie,' she says with visible tears in her eyes now and anger blooming her cheeks.

'No, don't be ridiculous,' Archie says, smoothing down his jumper.

Alice belts him full force across the face. Gobsmacked, Archie grabs her by the wrists to stop her going any further. She wangles out of it. The welt on his face is massive.

'I already know. She told me Archie,' she says, tears flowing freely as she slumps down onto a ledge nearby. Archie is silent, the red mark vivid against his now pale face. Tell me ye didnae big man. Naw. Not oor Archie. Not to Alice. He kneels at her feet, clasps her face in his hands and tries to kiss her. She pushes him away and he falls on his arse.

'Alice,' he says scrambling to his feet, and she can't even look at him, 'please just look at me, Alice.' She can't. She stays staring doon at her jumper, rubbing her temples.

'I was pished! I know it's not an excuse. But I was crying and making a fool of myself. Then the next thing is she's smacked the lips on me. But I did push her away,' he confesses, voice wobbling now. 'I instantly regretted it. I stopped it as soon as I knew what I was doing,' he pleads.

Alice remains in stony silence, as though his words are falling on deaf ears.

'It was just a kiss,' he says taking her hands and kissing them tenderly. She looks at him finally, her eyes puffy and red from tears. 'It was nothing like what we have.'

'We don't have anything anymore,' she says numbly.

'No,' Archie says defiantly, 'I've fucked up, but we're *forever* Alice.'

'You kissed her, which makes me want to fucking burn this whole distillery down!' says Alice standing up and walking towards the door. 'But when I asked you for honesty, you gave me lies Archie.'

The big chap doesn't know what to say.

'You can't even say anything,' she says, appalled by his silence, 'You've let me down in the worst possible way.'

'I would chop the next fifty years off my life if I could get another chance with you,' he says desperately.

'And if you ever try and speak to me again, I'll chop something else off,' she warns.

'Alice we can work it out,' he pleads. 'I'm so sorry!'

'So am I,' she says. 'Sorry that I trusted a wee boy with my heart.'

Chapter 19
New Chapters
Enid

I'm getting about ok since I've gotten out of hospital. I'm very weak, but that's the treatment taking its toll. My hubby's been the best, taking very good care of me. My son has been a god send, despite his broken heart. I tried to vouch for him to Alice, what a lovely lassie she is, but her mind's set. You've broken her trust – I tried to explain to Archie, but he's grieving the relationship so nothing will get through. Alice won't even talk to him. She still pops in to see me every day though, and brings me lovely lunches so I don't need to worry about food until Arthur gets in. The nurse comes through periodically, but I don't think I could manage without Alice and all her help. I hope one day she can forgive my boy. She is a shining light in all of our lives, and I pray to god that he brings them back together one day. Some people you meet are just special, and you know they're meant to be family.

I've even been managing down to the chapel most weeks. Father says he'll come to me, but I'm not ready for that yet. That time will come. For now, I'm plodding on and taking right good care of myself for my family. It's a proud day today, my wee boy is heading off to university. He tried to convince us to let him defer for a year because of my illness, but I was having none of it. I don't want to hold my son back. I'm very proud of all he has achieved. He's learned a lot during this summer, after graduating high school. His time at the distillery has shown him all that goes on to run the business. He's grown up a lot and working in the real world and earning a wage has done him the world of good. I still feel university will be the best thing for him though. It's nice to think that he might come back and help his Da run the business. But I don't want that to be his only option. It should be a choice. Arthur inherited the farm from his Da and made it what it is today. He established the distillery, but it would have been nice for him to choose his path.

Arthur's taking him up today with the van loaded up with stuff for his dorm room. I've made sure to get him nice new stuff, all fresh for his new digs. Arthur will take him for a curry after he's all settled in, before he comes back home to me. I've asked Alice if she'll sit with me today as it's her day off. She's coming round soon. There's the door just now actually. I manage to hobble to the door from the couch and let her in.

'Hi Enid,' she says, enveloping me in those slim arms of hers. 'I've got all sorts of goodies for us today and I brought a few DVDs and games we could try,' she says breaking away and taking her shoes off at the door. She makes her way into the kitchen. It's like second nature to her. She feels at home here.

'Och thanks love,' I say easing back into my seat and wincing at the pain in my incision site. 'That'll keep my mind off it all.'

'How are you feeling today?' she says, sympathetically, in the kitchen. Our living room and kitchen are open plan with a breakfast bar in between, so we can easily chat.

'I'm well in myself, but I just feel like crap that I'll no be there for Archie's big move,' I say flicking the channel to some music. I look at Alice to see her sadly packing away the food into the fridge.

'Och sorry pet, I didn't mean to upset ye,' I say feeling guilty. There's still a lot of love between them. If only they could sort it out.

'No, it's ok, I just didn't realise he was leaving so soon,' says Alice wounded. She hasn't allowed him to speak to her in months. She wipes away the sweat from her forehead.

'Take that big jumper off,' I say addressing the oversized sweatshirt she's wearing. 'It's roasting in here, but I don't even notice. I've got that thin I need the heating on constant,' I say examining the stick-thin arms in my own cardigan. I look at my poor wee knees sticking out awkwardly from my thin legs. I've spent my whole life worrying about my dress size and now I'd love to not have to worry about being too light.

Alice brushes off the comment, 'I'll be fine, think it was just carrying all the bags up here, that's some hill by the way.' She's all organised now and beginning to look more herself.

'Shall I start making us some lunch Enid?' she asks bringing me the bag of games and DVDs.

'Yeah pet that would be grand, I'll pick the movie, shall I?' I say with a wee sparkle in my eye. She always lets me pick anyway, she spoils me, so she does.

'Of course,' she laughs, and I feel a warmth in my chest. I never felt I missed out by just having a son, but when I spend time with Alice, I realise having a daughter would have been nice. She likes to watch all the same stuff as me, but the boys ruled the TV in our house.

I watch the clock as she preps the lunch, the boys are due back any minute. The key in the door signals their return and I can see Alice flinch as she busies herself with the cooking. Arthur and Archie stomp in the door.

'Eh, boots!' I say, the usually greeting they get from me. What is it with men, hell-bent on destroying a lovely tidy house with their giant boots? They obey with a smile and each in turn gives me a kiss. Arthur nods to Alice and heads upstairs to bring more boxes down. Archie looks at Alice in the kitchen, sadness filling his eyes.

'Go and speak to her,' I whisper, trying not to peek Alice's interest. She's got her back to us over the pot of soup anyway. She's trying to pretend she doesn't see him.

'She doesn't want to speak to me ever again,' Archie says stubbornly. 'Plus, she slapped me,' he adds.

'Listen, you deserved that slap!' I remind him. 'Don't be daft. Just go in and say hello,' I warn, because in all honesty it's an order not a request. He needs to make the effort. He's the one in the wrong.

Archie makes his way, uneasily, into the kitchen. I can tell he's not got a clue what to do. He takes a spoon from the drawer and takes some soup. Alice looks annoyed.

'Needs pepper,' he says with an awkward laugh.

'Big day today?' she says coolly, leaning against the worktop.

'Yeah, moving day. We've just got a few more boxes for Da's van, then we're off,'

'Well best of luck,' Alice says dryly.

'Could I not get a cuddle goodbye?' says Archie as he tries to put his hands round her waist and pull her in for a cuddle. She flinches away, protecting her stomach with her arms.

'I don't think it's a good idea Archie,' she says sadly, 'too much has happened between us.'

Archie looks wounded and I try to act subtle as I spy on their conversation. I could probably pass for watching TV, as the two of them are absorbed in each other.

'You were my friend first Alice,' he says full of emotion now, 'the best friend I've ever had remember? If you can't be with me in the way I want, can you not still be my pal?'

'I can't just be friends with you Arch,' she says tearing up now, 'I'll always want more. And that's not an option.'

'It is an option,' he says taking her hands. 'I never wanted to ruin us over one stupid mistake!'

She shakes her head.

'I should have been honest,' he admits.

'You're too young for all this commitment,' Alice says, pulling bowls down from the cupboard. 'You need to go to university and grow up and find out who you are without me. Because *I'm* not an option anymore, Arch.'

Arthur appears at the typically wrong time and announces it's time to go. The boys pack the rest of the stuff into the van as I watch from the door. I really hoped that Archie leaving would change her mind. Arthur starts his van and blows a kiss to me from the open window. I catch it and press it to my heart. Archie is running up the path towards me. His hug nearly knocks me off my feet. He squeezes me tight.

My wee boy.

'It's not too late for me to stay Ma,' he says almost crying, 'I want to be here for you.'

'I've got your Da and you're only a wee drive away pet,' I say reassuringly. 'I want phone calls and letters and visits mind. You go chase your future. As long as you don't forget about yer wee ma that's fine.'

'Never,' he whispers as he hugs me tightly again. He looks over my shoulder into the house and hesitates for a moment before heading back to his car. Then they are off. My wee boy is heading to university and starting a new chapter in his life. I wipe the tears from my face before I go back to Alice.

I'm sad I couldn't be there in Dundee to see him settled. I worry about what else I'll miss in years to come. I'm not ready for that yet. I'll just take right good care of myself for my family. That's all a mother can do.

Chapter 20

Bump in the road

Barley:

It's me again, Barley. I'm still sitting in the warehouse, no change here. But I notice a massive change in Alice, and *massive* is the word. She still comes here most days on her break, with a wee packed lunch. She kept her copy of the keys from when she and Arch would come here to canoodle. She's perched on top of a wee stool now, clutching at her back in agony. She winces as she tries to get comfortable. I thought she'd been hitting the chocolates to comfort eat over oor Archie, but now I suspect something different.

'Oh aye?' says Hoppo sarcastically. 'And what gave that away?'

She has unbuttoned her overalls; she's been wearing big baggy men's ones of late. I can't help but notice, as she slips her arms from the sleeves and ties it round her waist, that there's something different about Alice. She pulls up her tank top to rub her swollen belly. The bump looks like it's stretching her skin. She gives it a wee pat with tears streaming from her face and then covers it again. She wipes away the tears and tries to eat her sandwiches, but I can tell she's struggling. She looks roasting and uncomfortable and I feel sorry for her. But a wee baby? Surely that's a good thing Alice? Why are you sitting here all alone crying? Oor Archie would be thrilled.

'That's the thing though, Barley mate, she hasn't told him,' pipes up Hoppo. 'She hasn't told anyone by the looks of it.'

Aye, there's no way Archie's da would have her working away if he knew. It can be a dangerous place this distillery. Well it looks like she's told someone. One lone confidant who she's phoning right now.

'Hi,' she says sadly, trying to control herself. 'Have you got time to talk?'

I can't hear them on the other end, but I can hear her side of things.

'I burst into tears in the still house today, because someone made a fat joke about me,' she pauses to listen to the other end.

'I know,' she laughs, 'It's just my hormones are all over the place and I just feel so, so sad all the time.'

'I don't think I can go on much longer. I'm knackered, I'm achy and I can't concentrate. Plus, it's getting harder and harder to hide my bump.'

'I'm going to have to just resign, I can't tell Arthur. He'll knows it's Archie's.'

'He's not ready for this. I'm not even ready for this,' she says stroking her bump, 'but I'm older at least. I'd ruin his whole life.'

'What eighteen-year-old boy wants to be a Dad? It's not even an option.'

'I'm coming home soon sis, it's been months and mum and dad are hounding me. I think they think I've lost the plot out here,' she says brushing her fringe back off her forehead. 'Maybe I have.'

'I'll tell them then. I can't handle this on my own anymore. They can help. I'll need to move back home.'

'Can you tell them for me please? Tell them Alice is coming home this weekend. I don't think I can face phoning them.'

'Thanks Liz, and thanks for being there for me, always.'

'I'd offer you the same support, but the golden child would never fuck up this bad.'

'Of course, I know it's a blessing,' she says sadly. 'I just wish I could have given the baby the whole package and not just me.'

'Yes, a crazy aunt does help! I need to go sis, love you lots.'

Alice hangs up the phone and pulls her overalls back on fully. She hides the bump beneath the heavy fabric and people will be none the wiser.

Alice is leaving? Going back to Luss? Surely not Hoppo.

What about her apprenticeship? What about Archie?

Chapter 21
Resignation
Arthur:

Alice sits in front of me.

'You alright pal?' I ask, as I can see she's physically drained. She looks like she's got a lot on her mind. She asked for this meeting today. I'm just hoping she's no getting any hassle. It's tough working in a male dominated environment like this, but Alice is a strong person. In truth, I've always admired her guts taking the job here.

'Yeah Arthur,' she says in such a sad tone of voice that I'm really starting to get worried. She slides a neatly creased letter across the desk to me. I open it and read the short statement.

'I'm very sorry to hear that Alice,' I say, genuinely, when I have finished reading.

'You've become a real part of the family here.' I mean it. Despite how things went between Archie and Alice, she's been a model employee, and a great source of support to Enid through her illness.

'Thanks Arthur, I appreciate everything you've done for me,' she says with a small smile. 'I'll miss working with you all.'

'Can I ask if there is a reason?' I ask, as it really seems to have come out of the blue.

'It's too personal to discuss,' she says and it's clear from her emotional tone that I shouldn't probe any further.

'And there is nothing I can do to change your mind doll?' I offer, hoping maybe to gain her confidence.

There's always a way around problems, if only she'd trust me enough to say.

'I'm sorry, but I need a fresh start,' she says rejecting my offer, 'it's no reflection on the distillery, or you, Arthur.'

'Ok,' I say, not wanting to harass her about it. 'So, you're finishing up in two weeks then?' I say scanning the letter again.

'Yeah,' Alice says, with a big sigh. It looks like a massive weight has been taken off her shoulders already. Has she really been unhappy here?

'Okdoke, nae bother at all pal. I'll let payroll know and we'll get all your holiday pay sorted.'

Alice stands up to leave and I offer her a handshake. She shakes my hand firmly, but eventually breaks down. I can't help but sweep her into my arms. I know it's maybe unprofessional, but I've always looked at Alice as one of my own. The love she has shown to my Mrs, has earned her a special badge of honour in my book.

'Come here, you,' I say comforting her. 'You can always come back and visit us. In fact, I expect you to for my wee Mrs,' I say pointing a faux stern finger at her.

It's worked and I've made her laugh.

'I just want you to know Arthur, I plan on continuing my apprenticeship,' she promises, trying to compose herself again.

I look at her puzzled. Although I'm pleased she'll carry on her training, I don't know why she feels the need to assure me.

'I don't want you to feel you wasted time on me,' she explains.

'Not at all, doll, it's been an absolute pleasure,' I reassure her.

'Thanks Arthur. I appreciate all the time you've invested in me, and I can assure you everything I've learnt here I'll take with me throughout my life,' she says tearing up again. 'I better go, before I start greeting again. I didn't realise how hard this would be today.'

Alice leaves and I sit for a minute. I've got so much to do. The pressure I'm under is unbelievable at the moment. I feel ancient and knackered. Then I think about how gubbed my wee wife looked this morning. I feel like I'm in the wrong place being here. I just want to be with her. I pick up the phone and give her a wee call. No day's too busy to check in on my wee sweetheart.

'Hello? Enid, how you doing doll? I was just thinking of ye.'

Chapter 22
Letters
Archie and Enid:

30th September

Dear Ma,

As promised, I'm writing to tell you all about uni. Even though I'll phone you every week, I'd like to send you a wee letter once a month to start a wee tradition for us. You once said you wished Da would write you love letters. Well, this is the closest I can give you as you know Da's never going to be able to do that. So, you'll need to settle for your wee boy's words.

I miss home already, I'm half starved, and I hate not having my dinner ready for me when I get in. So, I'd just like to say thank you for that. I don't think I ever really thought about it at home. When I next visit, you'll need to teach me some recipes. I know you've tried before, but I'll actually listen this time. Campus is mental and I've got classes back to back and hardly any time to find the places. I've managed most of the lectures so far. My academic advisor is arrogant and not much support. If I ask him anything, he just refers me to peer support.

Halls is wild; they're bevvying all the time. I'm not getting in many places as I've not got ID. I'm sure you'll be glad to hear that anyway. But I've managed to get a few drinks and enjoyed fresher's week. I even kissed a nice lassie I met at the beach party. We've decided just to be pals though as she's still wrapped up in her ex. And well, you know my situation. How is Alice by the way? Does she ever ask for me? You know, I'm not even sure I want to know the answer.

Anyway, my room mates are weirdos, but we're getting to know each other. I kick about with Kayleigh, that lassie I mentioned, most of the time as we've got classes together and my new mates Gav and Michael from class too. It's weird how close you get spending most of the day with these folks. We've got all the same worries. Plus, they can sneak me pints. In between serious academic pursuits of course.

I've got my first essay due in 3 weeks and I'm bricking it Ma. First year isn't what I thought it would be on an English lit/ creative writing degree. This essay is on a general arts module and we need to cover loads of varied stuff from ancient studies to architecture. I feel a bit out of my depth with it all. I just wish we could get into the stuff I want to study. But I think it's to give us a good grounding, something to do with analytical thinking. Anyway, I'll need to start it soon as it's on cross-cultural encounters between Benin and Portugal in the 16th century. Yes, it's as dull as it sounds. One good thing is I'm feeling really inspired. I've been using the lectures as sort of creative writing prompt and seeing what I come up with. I'll email you some stuff through if you'd like a read. There's a creative writing group starting soon, and Kayleigh says I should go. What do you think? It's a bit scary putting your work out for criticism.

That's enough about me though. I'm thinking about you all the time Ma. I'm coming home at the end of next month. Maybe I could take you out for lunch?

Love.

Archie

2nd October

Dear Archie,

Son, I was so delighted with my letter. You just don't get anything nice in the mail now. But every month I'll know my son has taken the time to write to me. I absolutely love it. I will certainly train you up in the kitchen and hopefully some of it will stick this time. We'll start you a wee recipe book, so you don't feel so far from home. But you can't let it out of your sight Archie, family recipes must be guarded with your life. I'm not wanting some wee guy to make fortunes off my lovely meals.

I'm glad to hear you are not getting pished out your face every night. As you're not 18 until December I'd appreciate it if you just stayed away from it till then. But I know it's probably naïve to think you'll listen to your mother. Mentioning that, we must plan a celebration for your 18th, have you got any preferences? Kayleigh sounds lovely and I'm glad you have found some friends to keep an eye on you there. Good friends are hard to come by and should be treasured. I hope in time that you and you roommates can bond. Perhaps cooking them a nice meal one day could bring you close together. After all, my recipes never fail to please.

It's sensible for you and Kayleigh to stay friends as I think it's too soon for you to jump into anything new. But that's maybe just me overstepping the mark again. I know you're a grown up now son, but I still worry. You need to give your heart time to heal. Alice is doing well, and still coming up to keep me company when she can. She's wrapped herself up in her apprenticeship studies and never seems to be out and about for fun. I guess that's her way of processing the situation. She seems quieter than usual and I can tell there's a worry on her mind. I don't want to push her though as I've come to so look forward to our time together. I hope that one day you might find each other again.

The essay sounds hard and I'm no use with that stuff, but if I can help in anyway please give me a wee phone. You should get it started right away Archie, and don't leave it till the last minute. You only stress yourself that way. I'm glad to see you are taking some positives from the course and can't wait to see all the new work you've been doing. Please do send them to my email, and I'll try and remember how to work it.

We are both thinking of you all the time Archie and miss you so much around the house. Da's doing well and spoiling me as usual. Lunch with you sounds great, I'm sure we'll manage out somewhere.

Speak to you on the phone of course, but really looking forward to the next letter.

Lots of Love

Ma

Xxx

P.S. Jean says I should get Facebook so I can video chat to you on messenger. Stay posted for that.

Dear Ma,

It's great to get to chat to you on messenger, makes me feel like I'm home. I'm sorry I'll not be able to make it home next week to see you. There's a mini writing festival on and I don't want to miss out. I will be home in the next few weeks for a catch up though.

What did you think of the pieces I sent you? I joined the creative writing club by the way. I was wracked with nerves, but people seem to like my stuff. They do suggest changes, but I feel taking some of it on board is helping me hone my craft. I've started the first draft of a novel. I don't know if I'll ever finish it, but it helps me relax when the course is getting heavy.

Glad to hear all is well. I'm starting to get down about the Alice situation again. Although, I'm glad she's finding a way of moving on. Just when I think I'm getting over it, I seem to fall back into my funk. I really love her still Ma, but I know I've ruined my chances. What do you think I should do? I can't get her off my mind. Do you think she'll ever change her mind?

Love

Archie

1st November

Dear Archie,

Son, I know it's maybe not what you want to hear, but I think you've done all you can do. You can't force her to forgive. If you and Alice are meant to be together, you'll find a way back to one another. Fate and the universe work in mysterious ways. If you never re-unite then still be thankful. If the love you shared is as deep as you tell me, then you should count yourself blessed for the time you did have. Not everyone gets to experience a love like that Archie. To find a friend to love and a passion as deep as yours doesn't happen every day. But a firework can't burn forever Archie. Some things only have a shining moment in the sky and then they fizzle out. Me and your da, I know what we have is something unique. But I also know we'll need to say goodbye one day. I'm just grateful for the memories we do have. And I know that even when we are not together, our love will last forever. It's a bit corny I know. But people admire what we've got. And they should. Because I'm in awe of that man every day. If Alice feels that way about you son, then you'll be together again. If not, then don't be sad it's over, just be glad it happened.

Lots of Love,

Ma

Xxx

29th November

Dear Ma,

Your letter was almost poetic. Maybe you should be doing this degree and not me. I scraped a pass for my last two essays, I need to try and up my game. I've been writing to Alice too, but she never replies. I think it's clear she's made up her mind. So, I'm going to try and move on. For her to give up on me so easily, must mean she never felt as deeply as me. I'm just going to try and enjoy my time here instead of moping about over her. I'm sorry I've missed your last couple of calls, I've started a few clubs here and I never seem to have a minute to sit down at night to chat. I'm also working at the weekend in a wee bookshop café down the street so I'm short on free time. Hope you're doing ok though and keeping well. The plan is to get home this month, round about my birthday. Don't worry about a party. We've got tons to catch up on.

Love

Archie

4ᵗʰ December

Dear Archie,

I'm so disappointed you couldn't make it home this week. But I understand if you are feeling under the weather. What a rotten way to spend your 18ᵗʰ. I wish I could have celebrated with you. Is there a better time I could call you? Maybe you could tell me a night you are always free and I'll get you then. Da's always asking after you. You should give him a wee call or a text son, would be nice for you to meet for a pint. He's so stressed with the business these days, but he doesn't want to tell me and stress me out. It would be nice for him to have someone to talk to.

I've re-arranged the booking for the function suit at the pub for your belated birthday bash. I didn't want to leave it too late. Before you know it, it will be Christmas. Its booked for the 18ᵗʰ of December so that leaves us a bit of time left to re- organise. Let me know if there's anyone from uni you want to invite, and we can get them put up for the weekend in one of the guest cottages. I'll handle the invites for here.

It's good to hear you are trying to move on, but I think doubting Alice's feelings is a bit harsh. She did love you Archie, that much is clear. I know your angry at yourself but try not to turn that on her. Maybe one day you could be friends again. I'm going to invite her to your party. I know you don't want me meddling, but I think it's only right to invite her. If nothing else she's my friend. How are you getting on with your writing? Any more stuff to send me?

All my love

Ma

xxx

2ⁿᵈ January

Dear Archie,

Happy new year my darling, I hope all your dreams come true this year. It was so amazing to have you back home with us for your belated birthday, even just for a short while. The party was a great success I feel. I hope you enjoyed it too. Your friends were all so lovely.

I'm sorry Alice didn't make it, she told me she was under the weather. But I think it's still very difficult for her to see you. There's obviously a lot of feelings there. Christmas here was flat without you, but the parcels you sent through were lovely. That perfume is stunning, but you shouldn't have spent so much on me. Your da is made up with his new hat too. I saw your snaps on Facebook of your Christmas dinner with Kayleigh and the bunch. It looked fun; I hope you had a nice day.

How is the wee job going? Da was going to bring me down for a visit soon if you are free. You can let me know what suits you. Missing you.

All my love

Ma

Xxx

1st February

Dear Archie,

I can't seem to catch you in, you must be a busy man these days. How are things going? I hope you're doing ok with your uni work and not struggling. When are you sending more of your work for me to read? I've been telling Jean all about your writing, I'm that chuffed for you. You must get all your talent from me. Her son Alex's girlfriend is pregnant, so she's over the moon and knitting all the wee baby clothes. I can't think if there's any other gossip, but if I think of any I'll tell you when I call. Hopefully I'll catch you in next time. Or you can call me, I'm free anytime, bored out my skull here because I've been told to rest. Hope to speak to you soon.

All my love

Ma

Xxx

To: archiebhoy@gmail.com

From: enidsparkles@hotmail.com

Subject: Hello

10th February

Dear Archie,

I've been trying to call son. Have you lost your phone? I've figured out how to email instead. I didn't want to be the one to tell you, but you have a right to know. Alice has handed in her notice, and she's moving back to Luss to her family. I don't know her reasons, but maybe you could try and speak to her again? It just seems such a waste of the apprenticeship. Since you've not been home since your birthday, me and your dad were hoping to get through to you if I'm well enough in the next couple of weeks. Missing you so much and just hoping you're ok.

All my love

Ma

Xxx

To: enidsparkles@hotmail.com

From: archiebhoy@gmail.com

Subject: Hello

17th February

Dear Ma,

Sorry I've not been in touch. Keep missing all your calls. Maybe it' a better idea to email. I'm still doing my wee bookshop café job, but now I'm 18 I've managed to wangle a few night shifts at the student union. I get mega discounts because of it and my food free in the canteen before my shift. So, I usually go in early to get a scran. The calzones here are dynamite, so addictive. I've finished the first few chapters of my novel, I'll send them on to you for a read. I also got a short story into the uni magazine, so I'm starting to get noticed a wee bit. I'm so loving life here, I've settled right in. I'm still not getting amazing grades, but it's all general stuff just now. I'm enjoying the learning though. I've started putting away a wee bit of savings each week from my pay. I thought I'd get me and you a wee trip booked for the summer if you're up to it. I know you mentioned you'd love to see Florence. It will be cheap and cheerful, but I'll be able to take you, cause Da cannae afford to take the time off just now. I've not got much time to write this, but I'll be speaking to you soon. Miss you and love you loads!

Archie

To: archiebhoy@gmail.com

From: enidsparkles@hotmail.com

Subject: Hello

18th February

Dear Archie,

The novel is superb. I can't wait till you send me more. Glad to hear you are getting a wee buzz off of the learning. Anything that you're struggling with will come right in the end with hard work and perseverance. I am so proud of you. It sounds like you are running yourself ragged son, maybe two jobs is a bit much. You've got your studying after all and you need to make that a priority. Florence sounds amazing, but don't you be daft spending your money on me. Just you keep sticking it into your savings pet. Just come home and visit your old maw, and that's enough for me.

Buttons, the distillery cat, sadly passed away last week so we've picked out a new kitten for the job. It's a ginger tabby, I picked him because he reminds me of my handsome boy. I'll send you a wee email with some pictures. He's a character, just like you.

I know you've got a lot on your plate, but maybe you could give your dad a wee call. I think he really misses having you around. How is the love life going? I hope you're giving yourself time to heal.

Lots of Love

Ma

xxx

To: archiebhoy@gmail.com

From: enidsparkles@hotmail.com

Subject: Hello

23rd March

Dear Archie,

The police have been in touch, they've reached a decision and it's a heavy fine and a warning. They say this is the best case scenario, although they wouldn't really discuss it with me because you're an adult now. But you know me, I'm a nosey parker, and I find a way of whittling it out of folk. I've given them your forwarding address to pass on your verdict. So, let me know if you got that as it's quite serious. Da's going to transfer you the money to pay for it. Hopefully this is the last time we'll need to deal with something like this. I've left you a few voicemails, give me a wee call whenever you can pet. Missing you loads.

Love

Ma

xxx

To:	archiebhoy@gmail.com
From:	enidsparkles@hotmail.com
Subject:	Hello

1st April

Dear Archie,

I don't want to cramp your style and I know you have a life of your own up there, but I'm at my wits end trying to contact you. Can you no answer your bloody phone? I'd like you to come visit soon if you could. We've a lot to talk about. I'm worried sick about you. Please get in touch son.

All my love

Ma

xxx

Chapter 23
Ultimate Hangover
Archie:

The sun is streaming through the slats in the blinds and abusing my senses. I think I've lost my voice. I'm so dehydrated. I slap the phone for the 3rd time, rejecting the alarm. So thirsty, yet unable to move my body to get a drink. My face is still plastered to the mattress. Wait. I don't even have an alarm. I groggily sit myself up, staring at the gargoyle in the mirror. I guess beer goggles only work on other people. I'm still half cut and, believe me, I look it. I've not been rejecting my alarm. Instead, I've been rejecting my da's phone calls.

Da? Why is he phoning?

I catch it this time as it vibrates angrily in my hand.

'Hullo,' I manage to croak out, grabbing the water by the side of my bed. I spit it back out, wondering what kind of a cretin I am taking a gin and tonic to bed.

'Archie,' my da's gruff voice says on the phone.

'Aye da, how you doing?'

'I need you to come home as soon as possible, it's yer ma,' he says, and his manly voice has never sounded more like a wee boy to me.

'What's up? She's no said anything in her emails,' I say, sinking into denial.

'She's been trying to get a proper hold of you for months, Arch,' he says and the anger and disappointment bubble through his syllables.

'It's time to come home,' he says finally. 'Your family needs you.'

Before I can tell him I'll be down on next train, he's gone.

I had been guilty of missing Ma's calls, yeah. I've been too swamped to email back too. I hear the weak excuses in my head.

What the fuck have I done?

Chapter 24
Homecoming
Barley:

Yeah. I'm still here. Waiting and watching, letting the wood work its magic on me.

Oor Archie's back. Although, I wish it was under better circumstances. Remember when his wee mammy took no well a wee while ago, with a burst appendix? When they were removing it they found tumours had formed in other areas of the stomach and bowel. They removed what they could, and she's been on consistent treatment, hoping to beat it into remission. Well lately she's been feeling much worse, not even just treatment symptoms. Unfortunately, it's spread to her lymph nodes. It's too late.

Archie's home from uni to be with her and to support Da. Da's grieving for his wee Mrs already. He can barely speak a civil word to Arch. He's his target for all his anger, and Arch is beating himself up just the same. He's been coming here once a day to get away from all the tension. Mostly all he does is cry and scribbles in his notebook. Sometimes he'll read his words aloud. They're full of anger too. Mostly it's the silence he comes for. There's nobody to hurl harsh words at him here. He can't hear his mum groan in pain as the nurses try their best to be gentle moving her frail body. He doesn't need to listen to the word he can't really face. Terminal.

I'm happy to sit here in the silence with ye, Archie. You take all the time you need. Nobody's ever ready to lose their mammy.

Chapter 25
One In
Alice:

I guzzle down the water at 5.45Am. I have to drink a litre of it. It sloshes in my empty stomach and gives me the boke. My stomach grumbles, threatening, but the water drowns it out. My guts convulse and my heart palpitates. The rest of the family continue to sleep in their darkened bedrooms. I feel like the sole inhabitant of a planet far away. Today I will become a mother. Or today, I might die.

They've scheduled me a planned c-section, because I have low lying placenta which could be fatal to the baby if I deliver naturally. My consultant explained the obvious risks, assuring me I was in great hands and it was all unlikely. It's best for wee Peanut, as I've taken to calling baby since my first scan. Yet when I had signed that form, admitting my knowledge of risk of death, I felt like I was signing my life away. I'm trying to block it out. Time is going so quickly. My mum gets up and joins me at the kitchen island, her hair is a mass of wild curls and her eyes are barely open.

'I was up most of the night,' she says kissing my forehead and wrapping her big dressing gown round her.

'How did you sleep?'

'On and off,' I say, trying to hide my nerves for her sake. She busies herself with the kettle and zooming round the house getting things organised. I've had my bag packed and ready for weeks. Before I know it it's time to go. I kiss Liz and my mum and dad help me into the car. The pressure of the baby on my hips makes it difficult to walk now. Dad's driving and I sit in the front. He makes idle small talk, trying to hide his fears. I can't even concentrate. We drive through the ghostly streets, and I feel like we're the only people awake in the world. My mum makes anxious conversation, her form of prayer. She told me she can't live without me yesterday. We've pulled up at the maternity ward and mum is laden with all my bags like a camel. I hug my dad so tight and try not to cry. Dad leaves and we head off to the maternity ward on level one.

They buzz us in and direct us to a small waiting room. We're the first to arrive and I hope this means I'll be the first to be taken for the procedure today. Not being able to eat for hours feels like a massive deal to me. The white board has red scribbled writing, all smudged. It makes me think of blood. I hope I don't need a transfusion, as I've become anaemic recently. Maybe I am the only planned section today? Oh wait, no such luck. An older couple arrive and sit at the other end of the long narrow room.

'You have to have your hands out to your side like Jesus Christ,' I hear her say amongst the mumbling chat with her husband. The mention of Jesus on the cross makes me feel funny, and I hope she's not talking about the section.

I hyper focus on the messy white board. Triage. Why have the smeared words not been re-written? It itches at my organised mind. Is this a mark of the type of people that work here? Finally, the midwife is here. She collects us all, four mums by now, and takes us into a large, four bed suite. Mere curtains shield us from one another, but we can hear every word the others say. I strip and dress in the gown and mum ties it for me, tenderly. The bow is made from a mother's love. The nurse rushes through my notes, coughing and spluttering. I'm horrified. She claims they are all ill but can't afford the time off. Mum and I look at each other. These people are going to slice me open in a few hours.

I've hopped onto the bed and they are pushing into my tummy to feel wee Peanut in there. It's so uncomfortable. I don't know if it's a pee I need or just nerves. It seems so unnatural to let someone touch my belly this way, when I've spent 9 months protecting it from every bump and danger. They use the doppler to hear the baby's heartbeat. Now all the sing song voices are gone. The baby's heartbeat is erratic and fast. They are hooking me up to a wee machine now, I'm watching as it prints lots of stuff onto a long roll of paper. Mum looks angry. They're keeping us in the dark. Do they think something is wrong?

The nurse reads the paper and tells us that they think the baby might be in a bit of distress, so we've been pushed to the front of the queue. The surgeon comes in and shakes our hands and assures me he will take great care of me. A lovely wee nurse asks me to come and tells me to put my slippers on to protect my feet from the cold. The kindness shines from her face and she makes me feel sorry for myself. They all seem to look worried. Mum is dressed in her scrubs, and I laugh at her shower cap hat as I give her a kiss. I hope it's not a goodbye kiss. She has to wait outside the theatre until I've had my epidural. I'm terrified.

The room looks nothing like what I've seen on the medical dramas I watch. It's just like any other hospital room. I thought it would be all steel and modern looking. They tell me to hop up onto the bed. It's so narrow, I feel like I can barely fit my big bum onto it. The lovely nurse holds my hands as she speaks to me with sincerity in her voice.

'We're going to place an epidural into your spine now,' she says softly, making me feel like a wee girl. That's the way she's looking at me too, like a wee lassie.

'It's quite sore. But it will be over before you know it, and we put a wee numbing cream on first,' she explains.

'Ok,' I gulp and try a brave smile. There's a laminated picture of a hunched panda eating his bamboo on the wall.

'See that wee panda, the way it sits hunched over? That's what I need you to do. The needle needs to get right in between the vertebrates of your spine and that position opens it up for us. Can you do that for me honey?

I nod and do as I'm instructed, and I look into her eyes.

'Don't worry, I'll hold your hand the whole time. I'm here. Just squeeze really hard if you need to.'

Then there is a pinching feeling at my back. It's nothing like the pain I imagined.

'Well done you,' she says with another kind smile. 'You did great.'

She helps me lie down on the narrow bench. My legs are numb, but I can still feel my toes. I feel paranoid it's not worked. They are lifting my knees up for the catheter now and I'm assured I wouldn't be able to move them on my own. I breathe a sigh of relief. I thought I'd feel embarrassed, so exposed like this, but I just want me and Peanut to come out of this safe. Modesty is the least of my worries. The feeling of not being able to lift my legs makes me feel sick. It's like they don't belong to me.

They're letting mum in now that they've hooked up my IV. The woman from the waiting room was right. My arms are straight out a shoulder level, on arm rests that protrude from the small bench. It's such an awkward position and it hurts my neck. Mum sits just behind my head as they erect the screen in front of me. It sits on my chest, so all I can see is material in front of me. When I talk to mum it makes my head hurt, as I'm looking at her upside down. I try and talk without looking at her. I feel like she's miles away. I feel like my words are slurring, but mum says I'm fine when I ask.

I can feel the iodine being brushed onto my belly. I can feel it! Will I feel it when they use the scalpel? My heart starts to race. I feel them shaving at the incision area, then pressure as they slice, but no pain. I'm relieved. It must be happening now. I know they are inside my stomach now, as it feels like someone is doing the washing up inside my belly. They must be pushing all my organs aside to get to the baby. It's all happening so quick. I feel lightheaded now and very sick. The pain in my neck gets worse. Please don't let me die, I pray. They are pushing hard just below my boobs into my ribcage to get the baby out. We can hear suction, sucking out excess blood. There's no sound immediately, and then we hear a watery cry.

Mum and I look at each other in amazement. Mum peers over the screen to see the baby and instantly regrets it. She looks green around the gills as she focusses her eyes on me again. I guess the site of my guts open on the table is too much. I still can't see anything, but a team of people flood round to start caring for me. Their pumping me full of extra fluids and stitching me up. The nurse brings the baby behind the screen, all cleaned up and naked. I wasn't even thinking of the gender at this moment, I was just looking at my gorgeous baby.

'It's a wee lassie!' mum squeals, bursting into tears as she is handed the baby. Peanut is wrapped in a pristine white blanket. She's the most glorious thing I have ever seen. I ache to hold her, but I'm stuck in this predicament. A wee pink hat is gently place on her head; she's already got a bit of dark hair. She's got my nose, but her eyes are still shut as she gurns into mum. I can't stop crying. I'm crying happy tears that my wee best friend is finally here. I cry still more tears for Archie. I wish he was here.

'Oh,' the older nurse says, welling up a bit herself. 'Did you not know the gender? That's fabulous we never get a surprise in here! Everyone finds out these days.'

'We thought all along a wee girl, but everyone else said boy,' says mum gazing lovesick at my baby.

'Have you got a name in mind?' she asks me, beaming from ear to ear.

'Annie,' I say. The joy I feel is being overwhelmed by a fear that something is not quite right.

'I don't feel well mum; I really don't feel right. My necks so sore,' I panic.

'She's not feeling well, her necks really sore,' she says alarmed to the nurse.

'Do you feel sick?' she asks sympathetically.

'Yeah,' I say starting to cry and shiver. She puts a wee bowl at the side of my shoulder.

'Just turn your head and let it out if you need to honey,' she comforts stroking my forehead. She begins explaining calmly as they finish my stitching.

'You lost a lot blood, so we've had to pump you full of fluids. This makes you feel unwell, so I've also put in some anti-nausea drugs to combat that feeling. It will kick in soon pet.'

'Thank you,' I cry, as the shivering continues. Her words help me feel less like I'm dying.

'We're going to slide you onto your bed now,' she says, and they hoist me back into the comfort of my bed. Finally, they remove the drip from my hand. Getting to rest my arms feels glorious. But I still feel like I'm dying. The kind nurse loosens my gown and takes the baby gently from mum. She unwraps the blanket and places her naked skin onto my bare chest and pulls the gown back over her like a wee blanket. I can't describe this feeling. There's a chemical rush through my body. I feel something flooding through me. Relief. Love. Her skin is so soft and delicious next to mine as she nuzzles into me. She knows I'm her mummy right away. She loves me already, and I her. If I could bottle this feeling, I'd be a millionaire. The nurses all look on at me in sympathy. Having Annie next to me like this is healing me. I start to feel so much better. The shivering lessens. It's over. The dread of the last few months has taken its toll on me.

We are wheeled back into our room in recovery and I lie comfortably with Annie in bed. Mum takes first photos and starts calling around all the family. She can't stop crying. The nurse helps me adjust my bed so I can sit up. She places the baby in the cot so mum can dress her for me. I feel so helpless looking on as mum dresses my baby girl for the first time and puts on her tiny nappy. I'm still numb and can't feel anything from my breasts down. I feel useless. I pull off the gown with mum's help and put on my nightie from my bag. I brush my hair and feel a million times better. They bring me tea and they encourage me to keep drinking water.

'Don't worry, you won't feel like you need a pee, it will just happen and go into the catheter,' the nurse assures.

It's quite embarrassing seeing it hooked up to the side of my bed full of pee.

I get more cuddles from Annie and she seems to be rooting around for the breast. I ask for breastfeeding support and they say they'll be back in five minutes. I latch Annie on myself, and she starts feeding. I can see the colostrum running from her chin. With no-one to advise me I have to assume I'm doing it right. She comes back forty minutes later and says she can help.

'She's fed already, I managed,' I say proudly.

She gives me a wee sheet of paper to mark down first feed time. We wait anxiously to be taken to the ward.

~

I've practically forced them to let me out of here. Last night was one of the worst of my life. I've been given my own private room with a bathroom, which was good to have some privacy. The pain was disabling when the epidural wore off, and I've not been given any help looking after the baby during the night. They said mum had to leave at 8, leaving me all alone with the baby. She was so sniffly with mucus, I couldn't sleep. I was terrified something would happen to her. I've never loved anyone so much; I couldn't let her out of my sight. The control for the mechanical bed is broken at the bit it hooks onto the bed, so it slides out of reach. So, I've had to hurt myself, even trying to get out of bed to look after Annie.

I'm worn out and super emotional and I'm so glad my mum is here now. I've honestly never felt so alone. They seem to be annoyed that I want to discharge myself, but I can't do another night here alone. I need my family and I need help until I heal. I can't stop crying. I feel nuts. Mum says it's just all the hormones coursing through my body. I'm not so sure. The first night alone with my baby and I couldn't cope. Will I be able to do this alone? I've signed the paperwork and Annie's had her final check-up. We're free to leave. Mum carries the car seat and all my bags and I manage to make my way to the lift. I'm exhausted already and clutch a pillow to my wound. My body feels so foreign to me and I'm so afraid of hurting myself.

I step up into the jeep and instantly feel a ripping feeling at the incision site. I cry out. Mum panics.

'Are you ok?' she asks, wild with worry.

'Yeah,' I manage, crying again, as I look at my wound. There's no tears. 'I feel like I ripped something there.'

'Maybe we should go back in.'

'No, mum, please. I can't cope with that again. I'll be fine.'

'Ok, honey, let's just get you and your wee angel back home,' she says and plants a kiss on my forehead. I feel instantly relieved. We draw away from the hospital and I think of the night I had. I can't wait to be home.

Chapter 26
One out
Alice:

Annie is thriving; a wee chubby baby with the most beautiful eyes you have ever seen. She's like a goddess to me. The feeling of love I have for her is all encompassing, and it terrifies me. I think about not being here when she's an old lady. I worry that she'll be all alone one day, and I won't be able to look after her. I push those terrifying feelings aside and snuggle in her beautiful scent. I try to remain in the now, where I am her mother and she has all she needs in my arms. Does she really have all she needs? Will she grow up missing Archie, or even the idea of a dad? I know how much my dad means to me, am I robbing her of that?

She wants for nothing at my parents' house. She's staying with me for now in my room, but she's already got the most gorgeous nursery prepared for her. Archie always said he thought I was creative and that my sketches were great. I focussed this creativity into the artwork I made for her room. I've hand drawn and painted canvases for her room of all the lovely children's book and movie characters I love. She's only a few months old and already she's changed my life for the better. I feel like I've been waiting all this time for my life to begin, and now I'm really alive. I'm running on a few hours sleep and buckets of coffee, but I'm in love. None of that matters.

I got the sad news about Enid's passing. I am devastated. She was a true friend to me, despite my breakup with Archie. She didn't abandon me, as most mothers would for their sons. She was loyal to both of us. Enid was hilarious and perceptive and always trying to run your life for you. It made me feel loved. The world has lost a kind soul, and I think I'll feel her absence forever. I couldn't visit after I resigned as Annie gave me an impressive bump and I ended up not keeping too well. We did speak regularly on the phone though. I didn't want her to feel I had forgotten her. I thought about staying away from the funeral for Archie's sake. Why make him hurt more on probably the worst day of his life? But Arthur phoned me personally and asked for me to come. Enid wanted me to do a reading for her. I am honoured and terrified as I sit amongst her loved ones at her funeral today. Archie has not looked me in the eye once.

The time comes for my reading and I try and make her proud. I'm not religious, but I respect the comfort she got from her faith. As the final words leave my mouth, my eyes find Archie in the crowd. How different he looks. All the boyish looks of the past are clouded by his grief. His eyes are bloody red, tears glazing them. I can't help but cry as I leave the alter. I feel seedy for it, like this grief is not mine to take. I feel I have no place here. But I loved her too.

When the service is ended, we make our way to the funeral tea. Archie shakes my hand and plants a cold kiss as I enter. His eyes are like stone against me and I'm herded along as more mourners stream through. When it's all settled, I try to get him in his own.

'How are you Archie?' I ask sheepishly. What a stupid think to ask, I scold myself.

'Never better,' he says, and his words are cutting like knives. He remains with his back to me, in the open doorway of the hall. I stay silent like a naughty child. I want to touch him, to kiss him and comfort him. I need to tell him about Annie. Life's too short for all these secrets and to not have your family around you.

I touch his shoulder, but he shrugs it off.

'Look Alice, I'm in a bad place just now. Please just let me be by myself.'

'I'm sorry Arch, I can't imagine how you must be feeling. I'm so devastated myself.'

'Aye, so concerned for me,' he says, seething again, this time turning to face me. 'So concerned you've not spoken to me in almost a year.'

'I was going through a lot Archie,' I defend, trying to find the words to drop this bombshell.

'You abandoned me,' he says angrily. 'I fucked up, and I was dead to you.'

'You were never dead to me, Archie, I've thought about you every day.'

'Not enough to pick up the phone, or to answer any of my calls or letters,' he rages.

'I couldn't, Archie, it was too hard for me to stay away from you. I knew I wouldn't be able to have you in my life, half in half out. It's always all or nothing with us.'

'Well you chose nothing. While I was here alone, watching my ma fade away.'

I'm shocked at the things he's saying. I'm hurt by the anger he feels towards me. This isn't how I imagined our reunion.

'I supported your mum. We spoke on the phone, but I couldn't visit. I think it was right to give you space as a family.'

'Family? My da can barely talk to me. I had no one Alice. No one.'

'Well I had no one too,' I say, tears bursting forward. I think of how alone I felt in hospital. How can I tell him?

'You were here with my ma when I was at uni. Sure, you left eventually. But she leaned on you. You supported her. You were in my house looking after my ma. You took my chance to care for my mum.'

The things he's saying are ridiculous. What does he mean? What's going on in his head? I'm flushed and breathless, feeling like I'm being hounded. I try to remember he has just buried his mother today. Would he rather that I had not bonded with his mum and helped her as a friend? Why does he hate me now?

'I can't be around you Alice,' he says finally, and my guts wrench. I can't believe this is Archie in front of me. My forever. Telling me it's over.

'You are just a shining of example of the right way to do things. The right way to love. When I'm around you I feel like the failure I am in my da's eyes,' he runs his hands through his hair in frustration, like he might tear it out. He looks insane.

'You were the daughter she never had, and I'm the son who couldn't even answer her phone calls.'

'Archie, please just let me talk to you,' I plead, a panic arising. I feel like I'm watching myself drown on a tv screen with no way to intervein.

'No Alice, leave me alone!'

With those words he disappears back into the throng of people in the hall. I slip out of the hall and back into my car. He can't hear what I have to say. He made the final decision about us. I'm heading home to my wee girl, with a definite view of our future. One that doesn't include Archie.

Chapter 27
Back to Uni
Barley:

Archie and his da are here in the warehouse and they're staring right at me. Hi guys!

'That is a bit of oor family history there, son,' says Da as they eye-ball me. 'The first whisky you ever distilled.'

'Aye and it's a belter as well,' assures Archie. Thanks pal.

'By the time you finish that degree it will be officially whisky,' Archie's da says patting him on the back fondly. Archie's face is tripping him. Something's on his mind. Ye can tell yer da, Archie. Ye can tell yer da anything.

'I'm not going back Da, I can't cope with it. My heids all over the place with my ma,' he says. He looks broken, like all the light has went out of him.

'Listen Archie, your ma was your biggest champion. You've no idea how proud she was that you were away smashing uni,' Da says rallying him. Archie is listening to him now, so obviously the uni has taught him something. 'You can't let your ma be the reason you give up on your dreams.'

'But it's not my dream Da, I wasn't even sure about uni,' he says, and I think back to him hummin and hawing about it in the first place.

'Aye, but the novel you've written is yer dream,' says Da knowingly.

'How do ye know —'

'I read every piece of work you sent to yer ma too. I might not talk much to ye, or give ye compliments. But

136

believe me I'm interested in what you get up to,' Archie's Da sweeps him under his arm.

'And I'm as proud of what you do now as the first wee scribbles of crayon you did when ye were a wean. The ones that I pinned up in my office and boasted about.'

Awwww! These two would bring a tear to a glass eye.

'I think you sometimes forget that you're my wee boy,' he says, grabbing him closer.

'I want all your dreams to come true.'

'What's the point?' Archie replies.

'Finishing your degree makes you a better writer and gives you all sorts of contacts you might use in the future,' Da tells him. 'Don't be a mug, Archie!'

'I want to come back and work with you Da,' Archie maintains, stubbornly.

'*For* me,' Da corrects, laughing.

'Naw, *with* you. I want you to train me up as a business partner. I'll buy into the business.'

'You cannae afford that, son' he laughs, 'I'm no trying to be cheeky.'

'I've been saving steadily, working two jobs, Da. I might not have enough just now, but in three years I'll be closer,' Archie argues. He's got his eye set on this one I reckon.

'Finish your uni and come back to me and we can discuss it more,' says Da finally.

'Those are the terms.'

Archie nods gravely and they stand in silence for a long time. It's a guy thing, I think.

'Anyway, this barrel, I'm no bottling it at 10 or 20. I want to keep it as long as possible as a nest egg for you. When you take over properly it will be an old whisky.'

Archie finally cracks a smile. His Da does want him back here one day.

'Let's go home and get the brekkie on and watch the fitbaw. Then we can talk about getting you back to uni.'

They leave together, chattering about the upcoming match. Enid would be so proud to see them bridging the divide. Sometimes what you think people feel about you isn't always accurate. It just shows, it disnae really pay to be a mind reader.

Chapter 28
Prodigal Daughter
Alice:

I'm surprised to hear the familiar voice, as I shake Annie off me. She's attacking me with lipstick, drawing knots and crosses up my arms. I suppress my laughter and feign a cutthroat sign of warning. She goes to run away with that gorgeous giggle of hers and her beautiful white teeth. I snap my teeth and threaten to bite her bum like a big shark. She squeals and runs to hide. Motherhood is the business.

'Sorry Arthur, it's so lovely to hear from you. Is everything all right?' I ask, shaken by this blast from the past.

'Aye doll, it's just that James is retiring next year,' he pauses, and I'm confused as to if I'm supposed to know what he's saying. 'I just wanted to ask if I could interest you in starting back your apprenticeship. If you did, I'd hope to have you qualified in time for James leaving and taking on the role of still house manager.'

I'm gobsmacked. I've not heard from the distillery in four years, not since I left the funeral and Archie's life for good. Now Arthur's here handing me my dreams on a plate. I would love to get my career back on track, but I have the wee one to think about. She's started nursery so I've more spare time, but I couldn't move her away from my family. She's too bonded to them.

'I really would love to Arthur, but I've got the wee one now and I couldn't live on site anymore,' I confess, with my eyes closed in anticipation of his reply.

'Would you be willing to commute? I'll factor that into your pay and believe me the pay will be worth it,' he negotiates. 'And congratulations on the wee yin!' he cheers, and I can almost feel him smile down the line.

'Thanks, she's the best. I think Archie may have issues with that plan though,' I say, shooting down the elephant in the room.

'He doesn't run the business doll, just you leave him to me. If you want to come back, there is always a place for ye here,' he says firmly, quelling my concerns.

'Ok, I'll be able pop up and see you on Monday to discuss,' I agree, and we say our goodbyes.

I come off the phone now and grab my girl into a big hug, kissing her all over as she giggles.

'Would you be ok if mummy got a new job baby?' I ask. After all she is the boss around here, or so she believes.

'Yeah! Of course, mummy,' she says enthusiastically. 'I go to my work at nursery anyway, so it means I don't need to worry about you being lonely.'

This girl. She melts my heart.

Chapter 29
An Old Pair of Shoes
Barley:

'No, I'm not having it! You're talking pish,' Alice says, holding her stomach in laughter. Archie continues, unyielding, but laughing too.

'Seriously. How could ye miss that in the book? He's in love with him all along. The scene where he heads off with the feminine guy's place and wakes up to him in his underwear? That throws his sexuality into question, surely. The love story of Gatsby is between him and Nick all along.'

'Look, ye can wake up next to a guy and not be gay Archie.'

'I'm not saying it's a bad thing. I think the book's beautiful and tragic. It's a love letter to Gatsby from Nick,' he says defending himself.

'It's a bromance, you guys all love each other deep down,' she says shaking her head.

'I just feel sorry for poor Nick. Having to play along while his man falls for a woman that doesn't deserve him,' Archie jokes, and the pair continue to laugh together.

'Maybe that's why he paints her out to be such a shallow thing,' says Alice seriously.

'See,' says Archie, munching a big chunk of sandwich, 'I've got you right in about this theory now. You're so easily persuaded. What other book can I ruin for ye?'

Archie and Alice fit like a pair of auld sannies. I didn't think a few years back that I'd ever see them this way again. Book banter obviously is bringing them closer together. They've been meeting down here for lunch on the regular recently. I think they're keeping it platonic though, but the sparks still there. They're awkward around each other, like they don't know how to be without kissing and cuddling. Slowly, but surely, I've seen their friendship grow. Archie's even been introduced to the wean. He's still not got a scooby though. I don't know how Alice is coping with all this. I cannae hold my water, so she's lucky I cannae speak. I'd have grassed her in by now.

'There's a movie I thought you might like to come ruin,' she says grinning, 'I've got a baby-sitter for Friday if you're up for it?'

Archie looks uneasy, it's taken so long for them to build their relationship back up. He doesn't want to jeopardise it.

'As a pal, ya dafty,' she assures. 'I'm not going to jump ye in the back row.'

'You should be so lucky,' he flirts, and Alice blushes a little. They both choose to ignore it.

'Alright, I'll let ye take me out, but ye defo owe me popcorn *and* a hotdog for whatever shite ye've picked for us.'

'And they all say you're a cheap date as well.'

Chapter 30
Goodbye
Archie:

I can't believe I'm burying another parent. The big man hadn't been keeping too well, that's why he'd put a push on transferring the business to me. Something in our relationship had changed too. He wasn't treating me like a son anymore, but more like a friend as we built the business together. We were having money issues, and the stock wasn't selling well. We put our heads together and slowly but surely, we've been climbing out of the hole we'd fallen into. We've invested money in upgrading the distillery, making a compromise between old tradition and valuable modern technology. I think we've found a nice balance. We trialled our first distillery tours earlier this year, which were a massive success. We're booked almost every day now. Of course, I've had to employ guides, but the money we get in from the tours more than covers the costs. The things we have at our disposal now; social media, YouTube, Instagram - it's all amazing stuff that Da didn't have when he was building this business. We had started to put Ionach whisky on the map. We were putting our heart and soul into it. Da obviously put in too much.

A massive coronary embolism. I found him in his bed when he didn't show up for our meeting. I'd like to think he didn't suffer. A procession of people make their way to me at the wake.

'What an absolute gentleman your dad was. I had an awful lot of time for him.'

'He was such a character and one of the most generous souls I've ever met.'

'He just had you hanging on his every word, if he hadn't made it in the whisky trade, I'm sure show biz was he next stop.'

'Don't get me wrong, I widnae mess with him. But I respected him, because he always gave me the time of day.'

'I knew I could always come and find your dad, he was a confidant with great advice to give.'

'Although he was only ten years older and he'd likely kill me for saying, I always looked up to him like a father figure.'

'Aye he was so proud of you son. Always going on about his big handsome boy away at uni, but how you still wanted to work with your auld man.'

These kind words about him lump in my throat. The distance between us had closed since mum left us. How could we drift apart when all we had is each other? We built a new family together, with new traditions.

Alice has taken his death so badly. She's cried the whole day, and her wee daughter Annie is so concerned. She's a cute wee thing, usually up to mischief. I still can't believe she had a wean. I was gutted when I found out. I always thought I'd be the one to start a family with her. I see the way her eyes light up around Annie. Some things do happen for a reason. Maybe we weren't meant to be so she could get her wee daughter. I'm ok with that. As long as she gets what she wants, I'm happy. Because I will always love her, no matter how many years pass. She deserves everything I couldn't give her back then.

'I'm so sorry once again, Archie,' Alice's mother says, kissing me on the cheek and holding Annie's shoulders.

She's come along to support Alice and show respect to the family.

'You all made my Alice part of the family, please do come for dinner sometime. You shouldn't be alone,' she says genuinely, and I see the heart of gold Alice promised.

'Byeeee!' says Annie batting her eyes at me and fanning out her black velvet dress.

I kneel to her level and she swings round my neck in a big hug. She kisses her small lips on my cheek and says,

'Sorry you're sad! I'm going home with Nan, but Mummy is going to stay and look after you.' How I wish that was true, but I burned those bridges with Alice long ago.

Alice approaches and sees them off. I know when she comes back, I won't be able to face her. I slide out of the hall and into my car unnoticed. I decided not to drink today as emotions are running high. I make my way back to the distillery, to give my dad the send-off he deserves.

Chapter 31
Mammy Knows Best
Barley:

Archie's here in the maturation warehouse with me, sitting on a wee stool and toasting to his da's memory. He's two or three double measures down when he hears a familiar chap, chap, chap at the door. Alice is standing in the doorway, looking stunning as ever. In fact, I would say she's even more gorgeous after all these years. Her hair is coifed up into a French roll, with two curled strands framing her face. Her signature fringe has been grown out, but it seems to make you notice her beautiful eyes more.

'Can I come in?' she asks cautiously, and Archie steps aside to let her in. I can see him tracing her body with his eyes. I guess true passion never dies.

'Having a wee send off for my da,' he explains, handing Alice the glass to drink. She swirls it round, noses it deeply and then takes a mouthful. Then another. Then another. Archie moves it away from her lips, looking at her with concern.

'Right, calm doon with that,' he says, and his eyes linger on the droplet of whisky lingering on her lips. 'I thought I'm meant to be the one on self-destruct tonight!' he says with a laugh. It does nothing to hide the sadness in his eyes. Alice looks like she's bricking herself.

'I needed some Dutch courage,' she says stepping closer to him, and for a minute I think they might kiss. Surprisingly Archie is the one to back off. Is he clueless? He never could tell when someone fancied him.

'Dutch courage to speak to me?' he says as he drinks deeply from the glass himself, almost draining it of its contents.

'Ye can always talk to me, Alice. Ye know that.'

'Some things I just can't seem to say around ye.'

Archie finishes his dram and grabs the bottle to fill it up.

'Like what?' he challenges, barely even looking at Alice as he begins to pour another.

'That I've always loved you 1-1-3, and I always will, Archie,' Alice drops the bombshell and Archie's whisky gets poured over the side of the glass and onto his shoes.

'Shit!' he exclaims and wipes the side of the glass. I didnae see that one coming either Archie.

'Can you not even remember it was 1-7-3 we used to say?'

'I remember fine,' she says smiling and stepping closer to him. She stops when their chests are pressed together, and their lips are inches apart.

'You said you'd love me for one whole lifetime. You'd love me for the seven kids I'd give you. You loved me for 3 reasons,' Alice breathes, stroking down his arm.

'But we've only got one kid,' she says backing away from him and delivering words that take Archie down like a bullet. He all but collapses back onto the stool. He runs his hand though his hair. Alice bites her thumb, waiting on his reaction like a death sentence. The silence is unbearable. Say something, Archie! What are ye playing at? You've got a wean!

'Annie?' he asks in disbelief, voice faltering. 'You're telling me she's mine?'

I can see Alice frown and throw her hands in the air in frustration.

'Of course she is, Arch, I could never see by you,' she confesses. 'Did you think I just jumped into bed with the next random I found after you?'

I never understood how no one clocked this earlier. Alice mysteriously has a baby not long after splitting up with Archie. It's no exactly rocket science to know the paternity. Yet none of these numpties even bothered to ask her. Even Archie just assumed she'd met someone else after they'd split.

'I couldn't even bear to look at you after all that Louise stuff. I tried to forget you, but how could I when I can see you in my wee girl's face every day?'

Archie is standing up now, to defend himself. His anger has been sparked.

'Listen. You know that was the biggest fucking mistake of my life. But what you've done is worse Alice,' he says pointing at her accusingly.

'You're telling me now, after 6 years that that wee lassie is mine? Fucking hell Alice. I could strangle you!' he explodes, grabbing her by the arms forcefully.

'I had a right to know. You had no right keeping that from me.'

'You broke my heart; you lost that right,' she says as she remains in his grip. She doesn't want to move.

'My heid was all over the place, Alice, I was worried about my ma,' Archie says, covering his eyes as though to wish it all away.

'It's not an excuse, but you are bang out of order keeping this a secret. All this time wasted, when we could have been a family.'

'Don't talk pish. You were away living your life. You couldn't even make the time to come visit your mammy. What chance did I have?' she snaps, flaring up in anger

148

now. Seeing the hurt in Archie's eye's she crumples. These two would say anything to best each other in an argument.

'Alice you'd had plenty of chances, I begged for you to forgive me. But from the minute my lips touched hers I died in your eyes.'

'You screwed *me* over, don't you dare lay the blame at my feet.'

'But this had all started long before that kiss Alice. You started looking for an out the minute things went south with your parents.'

'Don't talk garbage, Arch, you broke *my* heart. You moved away to uni and you moved on like nothing ever happened.'

'I never moved on,' he says pulling her towards him 'every night I dreamed of you!'

'You probably had a different girl in bed every night,' Alice says, trying to sound fierce. Yet her eyes betray her as she looks at Archie longingly, his hands on her waist now.

'Then I'd lie there full of regret every time. I couldn't find anyone. I was still chasing after a memory. I was still chasing after you,' Archie confesses, and they can't hold back any longer. They share a deep kiss that seems to last a lifetime.

Archie breaks away first, the hurt still evident in his voice.

'You should have told me, I never wanted you to have to do all this alone.'

'I tried at your ma's funeral, but you pushed me away Arch,' she says almost in tears now.

'I wanted to share it all with you. I wanted to call you every time she fell or said a new word or made me laugh!

But you weren't part of my life anymore. You said it was over. You made that call.'

'You can't still blame me for that. I was so full of anger,' he says, looking tortured by the memory of how he acted. 'If I had known, well, I would have pulled my shit together for you and the wean.'

'You wouldn't listen,' she says pleading her case as the guilt of her decision to keep the secret weighs heavy on her heart. 'You once promised to kill any man who hurt me. Well, you hurt me most of all Archie. We were forever, don't you remember? You ended forever.'

Archie doesn't let her get anymore words out. He sweeps her back into his arms and they kiss. Their tears mingle as Archie begins to cry too. You would think a wee winch would cheer him up!

'If we could just wipe the slate clean. Forget who we were back then and what went on. If you could fall for the man I am today, then I promise I will spend the rest of my life looking after you and my wee daughter,' Archie says as he manages to pull himself away from their embrace.

'I'm a different person now. I was just a stupid wee boy who didn't know what he had. I knew I'd started to fall from the moment we first kissed. Deep down I knew you were too good for me. You could have had anyone.'

'I wanted you. You chased me. You made me love you. And then you ran.'

'I'm going nowhere now, not when I know what I have. I've got a chance of a family with you Alice. I'm not letting that pass by.'

They've melted together again and reunite on the warehouse floor. I allow them their privacy, but we are all buzzing they're making a go of it.

'I don't want to be without you anymore!'

'All we need now, is Annie's approval.'

Archie lies with the love of his life in his arms, his real life about to begin. On this sad, sad day he's been sent a lifeline. His wee mammy was right after all. I suppose ye should always listen tae yer mammy.

Chapter 32
60th
Barley:

Did you hear that? I'm getting oot of here! A big film crew from BBC Scotland is here, actually here in the warehouse where I've been maturing. Archie's being interviewed on his plans for us. I've been here for 44 years now and almost forgot that this was where it was all heading. I've changed a lot, I would say I'm a very sophisticated whisky now. I know hunners of big words and I've got the smoothest patter I know. I can't say the same for Hoppo, ye cannae polish a jobby.

'Shut it ya swine!' he says. Just you listen to what the gaffer has to say and try and not make me look bad on the telly Hoppo.

'I helped out at the distillery throughout my school days,' Archie says with a big smile on his now bald heid. He's the spit of his da without all that wild red hair. 'My father always wanted to instil a good work ethic in me and most importantly, a love of whisky.'

'Brilliant Archie, and what about after your school days did this continue?' says the gorgeous journalist in front of him. There is a whole crew of people hiding oot of shot. There's crewmen and Archie's family there to root him on. Alice is still a stunner, and man you ought to see the beauty that Annie has blossomed into. She's got a couple of teenagers of her own now, and they're all here to hang on Archie's words.

'When I graduated high school, I think my da was at his wits end with me,' Archie laughs, and the lady looks on in awe as though she couldn't imagine a man as smashing as Archie being a bother. She better watch those flirty eyes, or Alice will jab them oot. It took them a long time to get it right, and she's still daft about him.

'I was just floating about, not really putting in an effort into anything. I had no direction. My da knew people without direction get themselves into a lot of bother.'

'Idle hands,' she laughs in agreement.

'Exactly. I had applied to uni, but I wasn't even sure I was going. I was basically forced into learning every single part of the distillation process here at Ionach,' Archie confesses, with a wee look to Alice. It's where it all began for them.

'He knew there was a good chance I'd want to take over one day, so he wanted me to train me in his way of thinking,' he explains, hoping he doesn't look to nervous on the telly.

'That's really interesting,' she says looking at her notes, 'So, you really did every job here?'

'Yeah. It seems mad I know. But I did everything, from the harvest right through to the filling the cask for maturation.'

'And you learned from the process?'

'Oh yeah definitely! I learned more from that summer working with dad than I probably did at uni,' he explains. 'I grew up and took my first steps into adult life. I met people, and situations unique to this business. I was forced into new situations, formative situations. I didn't always make the best choices and I got myself into some bother. But that's what growing up is about. Growing up is the practice for messing up in real life, to remind you what your made of when the really bad stuff happens.'

'Sounds like you made a lot of memories here,' she says with a warm smile.

'Some of my happiest,' he agrees, 'I met and fell in love with my wife here. And some of my saddest memories too, saying goodbye to both my parents. But I think that's so appropriate for whisky. Whisky is all about memories.'

He can see she's not following. So, he tries to explain it better.

'The way it tastes is your knowledge of the world. It's why I can't tell you how a dram tastes. I don't know what it tastes like to you. Your experiences are different to mine, your whole life affects how you interact with that whisky.'

'You've lost me a bit there Archie,' she places her hands up in defeat.

'I give you a dram. Maybe you smell the sweet, rich sherry smell from a sherry cask whisky? We can both agree it's sweet and musky. But maybe that smell or taste to me is beloved like my granny's trifle,' he pauses to get his point across. 'But perhaps it's off-putting to you, because you remember being forced to eat something like that. Our memories and ideas about the world are always affecting our perception.'

'It sounds like you did a psychology degree,' jokes the journalist.

'If there was a psychology to whisky, I'd be a professor,' Archie laughs.

'So, can you tell me more about the cask your talking about today?'

This is it. My moment of fame. I'm coming oot to my adoring public. Archie has the barrel beside him and taps it lovingly on the top.

'This is the Ionach Barley cask. It's the first ever whisky I produced. I'm naming the bottling this to highlight the basic ingredient for whisky. Barley is where it all begins. I produced it way back in 2009, just before I turned 18. I'm now 60 years of age.' Archie boasts proudly. 'To honour my father, who passed away at my age, I am going to bottle this whisky this year at 44 years of age.'

'I would imagine it's very valuable,' she probes.

'All whisky is valuable, for drinking!' he jokes. 'The value does usually increase as the whisky ages. I feel the Barley cask is particularly special. We used a single cask of first-fill American oak, which simply put, means once this barrel is gone it's gone.'

'Are you going to keep a bottle for yourself?'

Archie pauses, thinking deeply about his answer. I'll stay with ye Archie, if ye need me to. Ye mean the world to me.

'No,' he breathes. 'I feel the Barley cask deserves to go out into the world. Every bottle. My mother once told me, that if it's meant to be the people we love will return to us in one way or another. A big part of my life is in those bottles. There is love in there. If I come across it again one day, then I'll take it back home. But for now, it has to spread its wings.'

I'm getting papped oot after all. No worries, my destiny awaits. Onwards and upwards.

'Great stuff! I would love to try it but coming in at £8,000 a bottle I don't think I'll manage,' she laughs. 'For those that don't know,' she says addressing the camera for the first time, 'the distillery's name, Ionach, is the scots Gaelic for perfect. So, I think we can safely look forward to hearing more about this perfect dram.' She turns to Archie again. 'Thank you very much for your time and we look forward to the launch.'

The interview wraps up and Archie and the family head out to celebrate. We're going to be bottled next week. Finally, oot of this warehouse after 44 years of captivity. I'll be able to see the sunlight again. But how am I going to cope without Archie? After all this time, I'm scared to leave this place. It's the only home I've ever known.

Chapter 33
Bottling
Barley:

It's bottling day, and my bottle is going. Our barrel has been rolled onto a big sink-type thing and we've been poured into a drain system. From here, we've been piped into a machine that fills the bottles on a conveyor belt. Hoppo and all the other boys went into different ones and it's just me in here. Wow! What a lovely bottle they've put me in. They've had it crafted to shape of a spirit still. Our label is deep purple with *Ionach Distillery* emblazoned in fancy writing. My name is the most notable in larger letters, *The Barley Cask*. Mammy, if ye could see me now. You always said I'd be a fine whisky one day.

They've bottled us at cask strength, not adding any water to dilute us. This is another fact that I hear the whisky buffs are going wild for. Whisky has enough water in it apparently. Alice and Archie are both here today for the event, and Archie is hand signing the bottles as they come along.

'This is an emotional day for me,' says Archie, 'just makes me think of my auld da so much, Alice.'

She links her arm through his and leans her head on his shoulder for comfort.

'He was a great guy, Arch. He's sorely missed,' she says, and I can see she's a bit misty-eyed herself. What aboot me, Arch? Are ye not sad that I'll be leaving the nest after all this time? Did I mean so little to ye?

'This whisky is probably the longest friend I've ever had, excluding you. This is where is all began for me,' he says, finally remembering me. 'I feel like I'm sending out a wee bit of my soul into the world.'

I'll miss you too big guy.

'That's the writer in you talking,' whispers Alice, kissing his neck. 'It's about time you put that novel out there too.'

I'm placed in my display box and then into an even larger box with some of my sibling bottles. They're all gibbering about where they are going. *Gordon and MacPhail, Master of Malt* and *The Whisky Exchange* to name a few. They've also heard some individual bidders have been first past the post and pre-ordered a bottle.

I wonder where we'll go I say to Hoppo's bottle?

'Suppose it doesn't matter about the destination, it's the journey that matters,' he says. 'And it's been an absolute pleasure to put up with your pish on this journey, Barley, mate.'

That's the thing about true friends. They'll slag ye worse than enemies if they really love ye. It's called banter.

Chapter 34

Flying the Nest

Barley:

All the other bottles have been shipped to their new homes. There's only me left. I've been bought by Sydney James. From what I hear he's a multi-millionaire from Chelsea and the head of large multinational health and well-being company. He's made fortunes from the diet industry. Basically people keep throwing their money at him. Slimming shakes, nutrition pills, protein bars, fitness videos and equipment; he sells it all. The full shebang. I don't know what he'll be like and I can't remember a day where I felt more nervous. Archie discussed delivery, but he's arranged a visit up here. He wants to look around the place and he's booked a tour. He's just walked in Archie's office after finishing it. I am shocked by his appearance.

I was imagining a well-kept older gentleman. Fit and healthy with tanned skin and a toned physique. Perhaps a fitness fanatic in his day. The man that enters is stooped slightly, with a visible limp as he enters the room relying on his stick. The golden eagle handle points it's deadly beak at me and Archie. I'm perched on his desk waiting. The man is balding on top, but the rest of his grey hair is slicked doon onto his skull curling oot defiantly around the base. He is grey in skin tone and in personality it seems. As Archie stands up to shake his hand, he snarls gruffly.

'Sit down, I've no time for all that,' he spits as he refuses to take his hand. As he says so he thumps his stick on the ground three times. He's like a judge with a gavel. I'm no impressed guys.

Archie is visibly taken aback. The man must be about 80, so he tries to give him the benefit of the doubt. He laughs and pulls oot the seat for Sydney and returns to his own. Sydney's face is tripping him and the deep brow lines of his face and heavy bulldog jowls suggest this is the usual state of affairs.

'Did you enjoy the tour?' Archie enquires, breaking the uncomfortable silence. Sydney's grey eyes squint at him in disapproval.

'It left much to be desired,' he scolded, 'for the money you charge the whisky provided is meagre!'

I can see Archie is offended, but he keeps a cool head and polite manner as he does with all customers. A quality he learned over the years here, where a younger Archie might have reacted badly to criticism.

'I see,' he says smiling, 'I can assure you, Sydney, that the pricing reflects the quality of the tour and the whisky provided. I actually run the basic tour, which you selected, at a deficit. As a businessman yourself, you know the value of customer loyalty. I try and make them all into ambassadors for my brand. The money spent pays itself back threefold.'

Sydney makes a grunt, signally he thinks Archie is talking a lot of shite. I hate the way he looks at him, the air of superiority is pungent around him. Do I really need to go with this guy Arch?

'Is this my whisky?' He asks, snatching up the gift bag greedily.

'Yes, one of only two hundred and seventy bottles from the Barley cask,' says Archie, 'all ready to go for you.'

'Thank you,' Sydney says curtly, pushing out his chair with his backside and clambering to his feet.

'Can I be nosy and ask why you came all this way to collect? I was happy to post it.'

'I don't like too many people handling my possessions!' he says exasperated. 'I'll be on my way then,' he says as Archie goes to stand up and see him to the door.

'Sit down, I can manage myself,' he snaps, chapping the eagle stick on the ground again in protest. His hunched form exits the office with me in his bony grasp. I swing backwards and forwards in the bag as he hobbles oot of the main office building and towards the limo waiting outside. He meets the driver with a grunt as he helps him into the backseat. I sit in his lap as we hurtle oot of the distillery. I see it fade into the distance as we start the long journey back to Chelsea.

~

Slap! That is the sound of Sydney's hand thumping across Elena's face. She claps her hand to it to protect herself from any further abuse. This is the way he treats his maid, but slave is a more accurate word.

'You are to go nowhere else on your errands, do you understand?' he warns before pushing past her and hobbling out of the room. For an old man, he's still managed to terrify and hurt the lassie. I'm sad to say this scene is typical of my life here. For two years I have watched this poor lassie in forced servitude to Sydney. She arrived here shortly after me, just a wean. Her passport was removed along with all her human rights. She's been forced to work here for this scumbag all this time. She's permitted out with the driver for errands, but nothing more. She is told never to speak to anyone outside. The alarm is set in the evening to keep her here. Her situation is hopeless, more so than mine because I don't have to put up with being slapped about by that creep.

If I could smash through this cabinet I would. I'd drop myself on his baldy heid. To sit as a bystander as she suffers tortures me. I thought I would be out in the world, making a difference, bringing happiness and helping people enjoy life. Instead I have to watch this misery unfold. I'm a silent audience to a cruel old man's violence. Every night I pray for a way to help her escape. Tonight, my prayers will be answered it seems. Elena has had many years to contemplate her captivity. Many years to watch his every move and wait for the moment for him to slip up. I think her moment has just arrived. If only she could take me with her, but knowing she will finally be safe is enough for me.

Chapter 35
Escape
Elena:

I pray that he will be here soon. Will Andrew be true to his word and come for me? I pray silently in the cold darkness of my small box room. The claustrophobia I have endured here has shrunken my spirit. I feel small, and many nights I have lain here wishing to disintegrate and scatter like dust through the vents. Where are your family you might ask? They are the ones who put me here. At twelve I was sold to a family in Paris, where I was forced to take care of the house and their child. That soon ended when Sydney came to dinner at theirs one evening two years ago. I could feel his eyes follow me around the room as I silently served dinner and drinks. Although I was not permitted to leave the apartment in Paris alone, at least I was safe there. They never mistreated me. Yet, I was still a prisoner. Mistress was always kind to me, and I secretly hoped one day she would love me the same as her own daughter. But I had a price and Sydney was willing to pay.

I was brought here to Chelsea against my will and assured that any attempt to leave would end my life. I was only 15 when I arrived, and I often wondered why, on brief trips outside, no one questioned me on why I was not at school. Looking older than my years ensured my invisibility. I walked amongst the living, knowing only a ghost's life. Unseen and forgotten by those I love. I have endured vicious beatings, always given with an excuse that blames me. Broken ribs and wrists snapped have been my payment for years of my life spent trapped in this house.

No doctor comes for me. No dentist trips to fix the teeth he has bashed out with the golden beak of his eagle. I do not matter here. Yet he will not let me go. Why would he keep something so worthless?

While tending to the outdoor chores and hanging out the laundry I came to know Andrew. He's the gardener, with a contract to tidy the grounds once a month. Our friendship blossomed through forbidden chats and stolen moments. I resisted at first, unable to trust as you can understand. Andrew's concern for my constant injuries and obvious sadness made me concede. I confessed. I needed help. He was horrified to learn of my fate. He has vowed to get me out of here and to safety. I check the watch I have hidden under my thin mattress on the floor. It's time.

I creep from my room in my bare soles. I dare not to wear shoes, and I step spiderlike along the floorboards that I know won't creak. They are memorised in my head and tested often. Sydney did not notice that I have replaced the keys he keeps hanging on his bed post. I clutch them in my hand, so tight I must relax a little as they threaten to slice my palm. The office is across the landing from the auxiliary cupboard I sleep in. The door is ajar, and I wince as it creaks upon my entry. I hide in the shadow of the room with my breath shallow as I wait for retribution. I am safe. He has heard nothing. The safe sits inside the cupboard of his mahogany desk. I find the key instantly; I've been memorising what each one is used for, waiting for this chance. I take my passport, my ticket to freedom, and a small bundle of £50 notes. I know it is wrong to steal, but Sydney has stolen years of my life. I leave the safe open. I don't want the heavy clink of the handle shutting into place to alert him.

I glance at the box sitting pride of place in the drinks cabinet. I feel like it's speaking to me, beckoning me. I liberate it from its glass cage and place it in my bag. I have nothing else to take, I have no possessions of my own here. Even the clothes on my back are charity shop finds selected by him.

I creep the long flight of stairs, my heart beating in my ears. The alarm code I have memorised. My soul begins to lift. Is this hope I feel as I hear the beeb, beep, beep of the alarm pad? Then pain rips through my head as he grabs my hair. I grapple for the handle and swing the door open as he drags me backwards. The crisp night air tingles my skin as I try to prise his bony hands off my scalp.

'You're going nowhere,' he snarls, pulling my face close to his. He spits in my face, and I feel sick as it slides down my cheek. He knees me in the groin, and I fall from his grip onto my knees. I wipe his disgusting spit off my face and clutch my injury. He scolds me with his sick threats, hammering his stick on the floor all the while.

'When you leave this place, it will be to far worse. Be thankful I have kept you so long,' he sneers down his bulbous nose at me. 'You could fetch me a pretty penny.' The tapping of the stick on the polished marble floor is maddening. Boom, boom, boom! It invades my brain. My anger rises. Andrew is running through the door. As Sydney takes his eyes off me to look, I snatch the golden eagle from his grasp. My anger beats him to the ground with the cold, hard metal. I black out in my frenzy of rage and wake to Andrew dragging me towards the car. Blood spatters my nightgown and I look back to the pulverised mess that is Sydney. His skull lies open.

I change into the clothes Andrew has brought for me in the back seat. We will burn the nightgown. We speed towards safety and my new life away from the confines of Chelsea and Sydney's prison. Many years of fear and sadness overwhelm my senses and I shake uncontrollably, and unable to quell my tears. Andrew kisses my head and assured me. No harm will come to me now.

'You can't find a person who doesn't exist.'

Chapter 36
Kyōto
Barley:

The events of that night will haunt me forever. Though I am glad the world is short one less psychopath. I miss those boring days stuck in the safety of my barrel now. At least I had friends around me. Even if it did mean listening to Hoppo's rotten patter. I feel isolated since we all went into separate bottles and scattered across the world. I didn't even appreciate it when we were together, and now I yearn for my adopted family. I wish for the days back in the field, where I didn't know anything about the real world. Ignorance was bliss. It's too brutal out here for me. Now I navigate this scary world alone. I'm glad Elena broke free. I hope that she can build a new life for herself, one of safety and love. I'll never know though. Andrew helped her get me into a whisky auction site and I sold for much more this time around. I'm a collectible. Maybe the money she made gave her a good start.

I'm almost suffocating inside packaging. I'm waiting here at the international collection office at Kyōto Post office. It's a large building, a buzz with people. I thought I'd be lost here in Japan, but it turns out I'm a multi-lingual whisky. I don't see that on my bottling note, but it is true. I hope who ever has bought me now knows how lucky they are. I shiver when I think about sinister Sydney. What a creep. I'm well shot of him.

Akiro has finally come to collect me. That's what he says his name is as he flashes his ID at the man behind the desk. I'm comforted by the warm smile the Japanese man gives the clerk as he scoops me up into his arms and places me lovingly into his satchel. So far, a vast improvement to that cantankerous old tyrant. We leave the building and the warm air hits us outside as the sun shines abundantly. We're headed to Kyōto railway station just a wee walk down the road. Akiro buys oor ticket and we only wait a few moments for the train to arrive.

I have a good look at him as we travel. He's dressed in a loose white shirt and baggy black trousers with no branding. He wears comfortable plimsole shoes, and an orange satchel across his body. He's probably about 60, but he is clearly a fit man for his age. His heid is cleanly shaven, and you could say he's almost monk-like in appearance. We disembark the train at Saga Arashiyama station. We are only a wee while away from Tenryu-ji temple. When we arrive, I see that it's situated in the middle of an astounding zen garden and surrounded by the mountain views of Kyōto. Akiro is waved the entrance fee, and I soon find out why.

'Akiro!' the woman at the small desk says. Her arms are stretched wide as she throws herself into an embrace with him, awkwardly, over the counter. 'I've not seen you in so long! Why did you stop the Aikido class?'

'Ah, Aimi, my hip really bothers me now. I am in pain every day. I can't give my students what they need.'

'Oh, my son misses you so much. I am so grateful for how you have taught him.'

'He is a good boy,' says Akiro, his eyes crinkling into a warm smile.

'Go ahead and enjoy the temple,' she says, and we make our way into the temple grounds. We head into the main hall. It's paper thin cream walls stand oot in stark contrast to the dark wooden beams of the building. There are no statues or shrines to be seen. The hall is very simple in design with tatami mats covering the floor. There are sliding doors that lie open to the wonderful garden. Akiro heads into the tranquillity of the garden and sits on one of the wooden benches of the seating area that overlooks the pond. With lots of people visiting today, you can see he can't get peace with his thoughts. He takes us right doon to the pond edge for a calmer visit.

The still water reflects the trees and mountains like a mirror; a busy palate of red and green surrounds us. Akiro removes a palm sized stone from the satchel, hand painted with intricate designs and symbols. He casts it into the pond, removes his shoes and bag and sits upon the grass. He watches the ripples stretch across the glass surface. In lotus position he begins to meditate. The breeze plays through the leaves, giving the place a music of its own. The peaceful chirruping of birds surrounds us. After some time, his meditation is complete, and we carry on our journey.

We leave the temple's north gate and we see the Arashiyama bamboo grove ahead of us. An immense forest of bamboo greets us with fenced walking trails travelling throughout. On either side of us the gargantuan trees loom. The walkways are lined with the tall, thin trees, which tower above us. The whole scene emanates a haunting blue colour, cast from the bark of the bamboo. It really does feel like we're in another world, walking amongst a different species. The atmosphere is so relaxing, despite the flurry of tourists and other visitors meandering through the forest. I wonder how Akiro can carry on with his bad hip. He stops every now and then, and I can see it begins to grind on him. Yet nobly he carries on. Could he not find a quicker route? Surely a bus would be kinder on his legs? Still Akiro pushes through his pain and stops every now and then in mindful contemplation of the grove. All the while I feel guilty as I hang heavy on his shoulders.

He sits and eats a small packed lunch amongst the trees. The air is so fresh here, and I feel in a state of dizzy relaxation. When he has eaten his meagre lunch, we continue the trail. The bamboo grove ends, and we follow signs for a monkey retreat. I am not going to lie to ye, I've never been so excited in my life. Monkeys? I've never seen any animals except the sheep and the distillery cat, and they were a let doon. I've never seen anything like this before. The hill becomes very steep and yet Akiro presses on, bringing us eventually to Arashiyama monkey park. How he climbed the mountain on that hip baffles me. I'm exhausted, just sitting here in the satchel. Akiro is at home here, not flinching at the signs to avoid eye-contact with the monkeys. I'm a bit scared.

'Enjoying your day off Akiro?' asks a large bellied Japanese man at the ticket stand. That explains his calm nature around these animals who, judging by the signs, could become quite aggressive.

'Yes, it's a wonderful day,' beams Akiro as he enters the park free of charge. The wild monkeys carry on their day-to-day lives around us. They are Macaques, Japanese snow monkeys, named for their soft white fur. Their faces are red and menacing, but the little babies are adorable as they scamper around getting up to mischief. People enter a small hut to feed them the appropriate food. The monkeys know to come to the wire fencing to get their grub, and visitors are wise not to feed them oot in the open. I don't fancy one of them chewing my face off. We pass through and make our way back down the other side of the mountain, back into main Arashiyama.

The area we enter is very touristy and Akiro stops and buys himself a bamboo and cherry blossom ice cream for the rest of the walk. I think it takes his mind of his pain. After rows of teahouses and noodle shops we reach a set of small apartment buildings. On the top floor we enter Akiro's humble home. He takes me oot of the bag and places me pride of place in a room that looks like a meditation studio. The walls are bare and, save for a Buddhas statue and candles, the room is practically empty. A small speaker sits on the window ledge for his iPod, which he plugs in to play the most relaxing instrumental music. Mats pad the floor. This is where Akiro practices his Aikido.

He changes into his Aikido suit, which hang lonely in the small closet in the room. He begins his practice, with stretches and deep breathing. Though he winces, I can tell he finds some relief in the exercise. Akiro moves like a ballet dancer, though his moves are aimed to disable an attacker. It's hard to believe this is self-defence. He is powerful still for older man, and I see the sinews of his muscles as he strikes through the air. He strikes his leg into the air and crumples in agony onto the mats.

I watch as my new owner cries. Akiro is man whose strength and skill once defined him, but now his health robs him of all that.

Chapter 37
Kaiseki Ryori
Akiro:

On the anniversary of the day that I became Sensei, I always indulge in a nice meal. Now that I cannot teach Aikido, this tradition seems even more important. I live a simple lifestyle, including my diet, so evenings such as these really are unusual and relished. I am not a rich man, but my recent inheritance from my mother's passing has made life a little easier. It allowed me to indulge recently and buy an expensive malt whisky, a drink I am fond of. I choose to live frugally in my daily life and allow myself to splurge on such luxuries now and then. I would rather this, than to feed my desires daily, but limit myself to a threshold of pleasure. Kyōto is famed for its culinary delights, none more coveted than Kaiseki Ryori. Tonight, I have made my way to *Kyōto Kitcho* in Arashiyama to experience this meal of many courses. I enter the building, and the atmosphere is serene though it is busy with many diners. I am shown to my table and can't help noticing the sorrowful look the waitress gives me. I am quite a sight. An old man out alone to dinner. Yet this is the life I have known for many years. I miss Emiri, but I know her suffering is over now, to which I am grateful. I am used to being on my own.

The ceramic black tables of the restaurant are all just above floor level and I find a seat on one of the comfortable cushions. My hip twinges, and I try not to yell out. Instead I am mindful of the sounds, sights and smells around me. I try to separate my mind from the pain. I feel the shiny table beneath my fingertips. I see the lantern flicker in front of me. I hear the laughter of couples nearby. The waitress brings me my Amazake and leaves me to enjoy it. It is made from sweet fermented rice, and I feel it enriching me with energy. I know I am in for a treat as I study the menu of the multiple courses to come. This cuisine is focussed on artistry of food and not on big portion sizes. It's a sensory experience. I imagine the colours popping from the plate, decorated with beautiful edible flowers and I salivate. The first course arrives, and I am not wrong.

The Sazizuke appetiser arrives, and I'm almost too scared to spoil the sight before me. Pink shrimp and soya beans in a deliciously sweet sauce. Its paired with pickled yellow paprika and white radish fanned out on the plate, and seasoned small fish. I eat the tiny portion, relishing in the explosion of flavours on my palate. Next, we have the Mukozuki course, and I am presented with seasonal sashimi. Maguro and Hamachi, sit on a bed of ice. Their pink and white flesh is meaty in texture and contrasts with the beautiful green plants around it. Cooling cucumber and fresh red cabbage mingle with the soya sauce mousse the restaurant has created. Next, Agemono, a course of lightly fried foods in tempura batter. The spice of the chilli dipping sauce nips my tongue, but the light tempura batter feeds a need on my palate for something less heavy than the course before.

I am offered a short rest before we continue, which I graciously accept and make my way out to the restaurant garden for some fresh air. My hip creaks in the socket. They have a beautiful lotus pond and a small zen garden here and outdoor lanterns light the pathways. Long, decorative grasses dominate, and cherry blossoms weep into the pond. I take a cigar from my satchel and smoke it.

It seems a ridiculous thing to do, when you claim to want fresh air, yes. However, this is also an important tradition on my anniversary as Sensei. I extinguish the cigar and make my way back to the table, with the smoke still coating my tongue.

It's not long before the Takiawase course is presented. Simmered mountain yam, shiitake mushroom, long beans, pumpkin, white radish, and carrot with grated yuzu garnish. Its exquisite. Futamono arrives, and I'm given a thick broth made of steamed yam with gingko nut and grilled anago, topped with popped rice and ankake. Then I devour Yakimono of broiled fish and pickled ginger. Five more luxury dishes arrive, and the meal's finale is the most delectable of all. Kiwi ice cream. I am packed full, despite the small sizes and my palate is exhausted. The evening has passed so quickly. After a brief rest I pay my bill. It is a sizeable portion of my meagre monthly income, but tonight is a celebration, so I do not care.

As I enter the darkened streets of Arashiyama, I feel like someone is watching me. As sensei, my senses are acute and alert to most dangers that may present themselves. I subtly scan the area and see two young males, with hoods erected studying me from across the street at a newsagent. As I make my way to the bus stop, I feel them approach me. They drag me into the alleyway beside me. I go freely. I do not live a life of confrontation, but simply defend myself when needed.

'Give us your money, old man,' warns one, flicking the tongue of an army knife at my belly. They have seen me at the expensive restaurant, assuming I am wealthy. The other boy tries to snatch my satchel from me. I grip it tightly and block the blow to my face. He leaves his waist exposed and I attack, knocking him to the ground. His friend presses the

174

knife to the back of my neck, threatening me again. I disarm him and throw the knife down the alley. His next attack lands him on his back. My hip throbs in its socket, but I cannot slow down. Always defensive, my aikido moves block my attackers and keep them from doing me serious harm. But I am an old man, and I cannot go on much further. The stubborn one, regains the knife and begins backing me into the wall. His partner strikes my leg away and I fall on my hip on the ground. I face my death here in a dark alley, on the night I became sensei. Blue lights flash my salvation, and the boys scamper down the other end of the alley and into the night.

I wait on the cold ground for the officers to help me. They scold me for not being more careful. However, I will not let pain or age dictate my actions and I will not let fear control me. I remember the day I earned the title of Sensei. I recall all the pain I have endured for my art. For this reason, I know I can endure this daily plague upon me and anything else life deals, through the harmony of mind, body and spirit. Mind and spirit will overcome. Mind and spirit will endure.

Chapter 38
These Four Walls
Barley:

I'm in Paris, the city of love, and all this lassie wants to do is clean all day. I thought I'd maybe be in a hip flask sailing down the Seine or swanning down the Champs-Élysées on a shopping spree. Perhaps taking in the sights of the *Moulin Rouge*. But no. She's got me lined up in a pristine cabinet next to other whiskies, organised alphabetically, by distillery name. None of them open might I add. There's a lot of expensive stuff up here. Yet I've never seen Julia drink.

I miss Akiro, at least he was entertaining to watch during his Aikido practice, and he took me to see the monkeys that day. He decided to sell me on auction and pay for a much-needed hip operation. When I first arrived, a few years back, Julia made the delivery man leave me on the mat and got him to send the signature machine through the cat flap. She disnae even have a cat! She just disnae like to have contact with people. All her food and clothes get delivered and left in neat piles at the door. She waits till the coast is clear and then sneaks out to get them. God forbid she encounter one of the neighbours. I think she's just about got over the eye-contact with number 7 last year. Almost. They remain named after their apartment numbers, and probably always will do.

Julia's home is amazing. It's directly overlooking the Seine river and flows open plan with massive floor to ceiling windows on one side. Everything is pristine, white and spotless. All her furniture is made of glass. The whole place shines like a crystal. Her décor is minimalist and chic, right down to the sole large leafy green houseplant by the door. It lies in a heavy marble pot and is the only living thing to come close to my owner in years. Even the floor shines high gloss throughout. You could eat off it. Which she wouldn't obviously, it might throw off her routine. She lives and dies by the routine, oor Julia.

Every day she gets up at 6am and eats the same breakfast of porridge, bananas and honey with a steaming black coffee. Then she cleans. She showers shortly before work, which she begins promptly at 9, always. Her desk lies directly beside my cabinet. She works from home as a translator. She finishes every day at 1 for the same rotation of lunches, week after week. After lunch she returns to her post until 4. She finishes for the evening and prepares the same rotation of evening meals. For the rest of the evening she cleans. The massive glass windows would make you sick being up so high. Julia doesn't see anything past the glass, it's like Paris isn't even there. She goes to bed at the same time every night without fail.

If the loneliness she feels is half of mine, here alone in Paris, my heart breaks for her. I wonder what made my new owner this way. In the two years I've been here, she's never even had a visitor. And I'd be shocked to say she's been any further than the reception of the apartment building in all this time. Her sister phones once a week, from Bearsden, always on a Sunday at Julia's request. I think Julia keeps her at arm's length, claiming she's too swamped with work or away travelling when Anna wants to visit. She's made a beautiful prison for herself here, high above Paris. Unfortunately, I'm stuck here with her.

To afford an apartment like this, she must be well off. Her translation gig pays fine, but I know she's a pro at hunting for rare whisky on the auctions and selling it on for a tidy profit. She knows her stuff, despite not being a drinker. Truth be told, I admire her work ethic. She's definitely a grafter. I just don't know how much longer I can cope. A whisky needs to live vicariously through its owner. But for now, we just exist, as life ticks by beside us.

Something is different today when Anna phones, to speak about the kids and Sean and the gossip back home. Instant pandemonium ensues and I see Julia getting stressed out.

'What were his friends doing while that happened to him?' she explodes, a mixture of emotions floods her face. Anger and fear. She begins firing up the laptop instantly as she shoulders the phone to her ear.

'You trust them all to look out for each other, but they're all just selfish little bastards!' she rages, lip trembling now with the threat of tears.

'Intensive care?' she gasps, and she looks fit to feint. Her cursor hovers over flights to Glasgow, unable to fully commit. Glasgow is thousands of miles away. Glasgow is outside.

'I'll do everything I can,' I hear her say, shortly before the call has ended. Sitting at her desk moments later I can already see her talking herself out of it. She pings the nylon tights of her left leg and then right repeatedly, caught on loop.

Something serious must have went down back home, because I've just seen something, I never thought Julia capable of. PayPal has confirmed her payment for the flight. She's going home.

Chapter 39

The Loneliness of Paris

Julia:

I wake up in his bed, naked. It's obvious we've had sex from the aching I feel below. I'm horrified. I don't remember any of it. Jean is my friend, well work colleague, and I've never looked at him that way. I was too drunk at the office party and I hazily try and piece it all together as I scan the room for my clothes. They're all scattered across the room, which is so unlike me. I'm a bit nutty when it comes to order and looking at the disarray upsets me. Why would I undress that way? I say as I pull on my underwear and dress with heart acting like a battering ram to my chest. I'm quick. I don't want him to see me naked. But that's just it. I didn't undress that way. Jean had done it for me. Stripping them from my unconscious frame like a child with a birthday present. I shudder as I draw the cover back over the exposed bed.

I creep into the living room, praying he is not there. The shame of the morning after consumes me. How will I face him? He's nowhere to be seen. Saturday is gym day for Jean, so he wouldn't miss that. I see the couch I'd passed out on last night and the blanket that I'd pulled over for comfort as I close the door on this place. He'd poured me into the taxi, insisting I was too drunk to sleep in my apartment alone. I would be safer at a friend's house. As I sit on the metro back to my apartment in last night's outfit, head banging, my memory regains its strength.

'Come on, Julia,' he'd urged to me in my deep sleep, trying to pull my unresponsive arm.

'You'll not sleep well there, come to my bed,' he ordered, as I remained dead to the world. I vaguely remember my quiet pleas of 'put me down, let me sleep!' as he carried my limp form to the bed. Then nothing else. Until I woke up naked and feeling violated this morning. I didn't want this. I was too drunk to say no, but my unconsciousness body should have been enough to stop him. Instead it gave him all the permission he needed. I begin to shudder and shake on the underground, growing increasingly cold. The people around me ignore the emotion ripping through my body. It's uncomfortable for them. I am just another nameless stranger in Paris.

I tell myself it would be easier if it had been a stranger, and not someone I trusted. There is an extra betrayal here. But really, there is no easy way out. No one should be subjected to that. Nothing would make it easier. On auto pilot I take myself to the clinic. In yesterday's party gear, those around silently judge me. They see a silly girl, too horny to use protection. After an interview about my sexual behaviours I am given the morning after pill. Then I'm screened for all the sexual health checks. The speculum is harsh against me, another violation to endure. I tell her nothing of the encounter. I can't say the words.

~

After the attack, things changed. It took me a long time to acknowledge it as an attack. I never got to confront Jean about that night, because over that weekend I'd become the office fodder for gossip. Our hot encounter was on everyone's lips as Jean told them of the hook-up. No one

180

batted an eyelid. Inseparable at work, they'd all assumed we'd get together soon enough. Jean was high-fived. I was treated like the office slut. The way he interacted with me at work, like nothing had happened, it made me feel sick. I shrunk into myself, beaten down by the constant gossip at my expense. Leaving the house became a daily battle. Eventually I became so crippled by the outside world that I had to resign. Eventually I locked myself away in the safety of my glass nest up here. Even the accidental brush of a stranger's hand on the train was enough to send me reeling into a panic attack. It wasn't enough to be away from Jean. I had to be away from everything, in a place I controlled.

Something like this happening was inconceivable to a younger Julia. Life came easily to me, like I had some sort of cheat code. I grew up in Bearsden, attended one of Scotland's finest private schools and made my way easily to Glasgow University. I made plans of being an international mediator, studying a Ba in French and Italian. I completed my postgrad in international mediation at Strathclyde and graduated with distinction. I was snapped up by a huge whisky trading company and hired for their office in Paris. I was happy to move back here. I had completed my year abroad here for my degree. Being away from home in a foreign place didn't scare me. In fact, it exhilarated me. When I was walking the streets of Paris with my latte in hand, I was truly happy.

I rented crappy apartments until I rose through the company, landing one of their biggest clients and distributors. Then it was onto this place, my sanctuary above the crowd below. I didn't know when I signed the rental agreement it would later become my cocoon. I clean it obsessively, not though fear of germs, but as a way to control my feelings. I clean, clean, clean, but I still feel useless. Paris means loneliness to me. What good is it to live in one of the most beautiful cities in the world if your too scared to leave your own four walls?

I haven't been home in years. In fact, I'd probably be unrecognisable to them now. My little brother is in intensive care, knocked down on a night out of heavy drinking. I need to get back home. I lock the door and stand staring at the keys in my hand for a moment. The familiar breathless feeling starts to take over my body. Then I think of Daniel, in hospital struggling to hold onto a life that I'm wasting. His big sister should be there to give him a hard time when he wakes up. I cross the small landing to my neighbour number 7 and summon the courage to knock on the door.

He answers with a surprised, but friendly, 'Hello!'

'I will be out of town for a while,' I say, voice shaking and with my biggest and brightest smile. 'Would you be able to water my plant for me?' I plead, like it is the biggest request in the world. He laughs as he takes the keys. Our fingertips touch accidentally.

'Anytime!' he says with kindness. 'That's what neighbours are for.'

Chapter 40
Texas Hold'em
Barley:

'Do you really think you need another glass?' Tuck's southern drawl snipes at Audrey. His belly rebels against his tight shirt, threatening to pop the buttons right off and take someone's eye out. That's the closest he'd come to a real gunfight, despite his complete absorption of the cowboy life. Audrey places the wine back in the chiller, and instead sips from her water glass.

'They say wine's the reason all you middle aged gals are getting fat,' he says adding insult to injury. He slices at his T-bone steak and shoots her a broad smile as he crunches it in his jaws. Audrey tries to smile back and make polite chat, to try and change his mood. He's stretching for the bottle now and draining it into his own glass.

'Your suit's all ready to go for tomorrow, honey,' Audrey says toying with her blonde hair. 'I can't believe René and Teddy's wedding is here already.'

'Now *she's* a fine-looking woman,' he says, wiping his face free of steak juice and relaxing back into his chair. Audrey shrinks into herself. She's a stunning lassie, almost 6ft with a catwalk model's frame and Hollywood bombshell looks. How she ended up with Wayne Tucker I don't know as I watch his heavy frame put extra strain on the chair. Other people might assume it's his wealth and the enormous ranch he owns, but I've been here a long time now. I know this woman. She's not as vapid as all that. She must have loved Tuck once, swept up in his charm. After years together, he's not so charming.

The housekeeper comes to clear their dinner plates, and he doesn't acknowledger her, but Audrey is lovely as ever to her. Tuck is glued to his phone as he gulps doon wine. I see Audrey start to twitch uncomfortable across the table. He laughs oot loud and can't wipe the leery smile from his lips. He tosses the phone down and makes his way oot of the room. He's away for his after-dinner cigar on the porch. His phone flashes across the table. Its inches away from Audrey's hands and she can't resist. I know that's why he put it there. I've seen him flaunt his affairs in front of her many times. I can only imagine the picture she sees. Her expression is one of defeat, and she keeps the phone tight in her hands as he returns.

'I see you couldn't help yourself,' he says in a calm voice, as he sits back down in his seat.

'Maybe if you weren't so insecure, I wouldn't need to look elsewhere.' His vile words don't even affect her anymore. I've watched him strip her doon over the years.

'Who is this?' she asks, her voice isn't one of anger like you'd expect. It's a weary one.

'Danielle,' he says, standing by the drinks cart now and pouring himself a generous bourbon. 'I planned on telling you after the wedding. I didn't want to spoil my best friend's day.'

Audrey nods in defeat. She wouldn't want to spoil it either.

'But as one marriage begins, another will end,' he explains, fixing her with his cold stare.

'I've had the papers drawn up and I want you out of this place by the end of the week.'

'So, you've been thinking about this for a while?' she asks faintly.

'I just don't love you anymore. Maybe I never loved you,' he says and for the first time I see a real emotional reaction from Audrey. She's in pain. It's maddening. Ye can do so much better than this clown Audrey. A butterfly disnae belong with a slug!

'Danielle is such a strong and confident person. I don't need to protect her or worry about her fragile nerves.' He looks straight at the long scar running up Audrey's wrist. Her pearl cuff bracelet only daws attention to it, unable to hide the full extent.

'She makes me feel great,' he digs at Audrey. For now, she makes you feel great Tuck, but soon you'll find ways to pick at her soul too. Ye cannae help yerself.

'I'll settle you up with the money I know you'll try and turn me over for, but it will be worth every penny to rid myself of the dead weight,' he sneers down at her and drains his bourbon.

'Well, goodnight Audrey, I have to get some rest. I have my best man's speech tomorrow.'

Tuck leaves Audrey, stunned, at the table. To be free of this fat and cruel big bastard is something I've dreamed for her. Yet she looks terrified.

Chapter 41
Wedding
Audrey:

My mamma named me Audrey after Audrey Hepburn. I was her little star. I lived the life of a southern belle; winning beauty pageants and finally making my way to Los Angeles to crack into the acting business. Perhaps my flair for the dramatic was what attracted me to Tuck. Wayne Tucker, my husband. Who I can now see flirting with the waitress as she hands him a drink for the first toast to our two best friends' nuptials. I'd like to say this is just my imagination and, believe me, for years Tuck convinced me of such. But I've had enough troubled trips to the gynaecologist to know that Tuck will never be faithful to me.

We met at a club, when Tuck was in L.A for business. He was a tall drink of water back then and I was flattered when he kidnapped me away from my friends for the evening. He chased me, making me feel like the most wonderful woman alive. He made all my romanticised dreams of courting come true, like something out of the Hollywood movies I was raised on. I fell deep and hard and into a whirlwind engagement and finally into a marriage that I thought was made in heaven. Over the years my rose-tinted spectacles have been removed.

His cruelty developed over time, but Tuck would probably be appalled to hear himself described so. He is a great guy. Everything in himself he didn't like, became a target in me. That's why my weight is always up for discussion as he has slowly ballooned over the years. I still loved him regardless. I kept myself slim for Tuck. He questions my loyalty yet flaunts his many lovers in my face at every turn. It's my fault of course. Look at me. Listen to me. Why would anyone want to be around someone like me? I've followed Tuck around for most of my life now, a glutton for punishment. I even followed him right into a psychiatric unit after trying to cut the imperfection out of my wrist. Trying to let the Audrey out of me. I guess I really am crazy like he has always warned me. What was intense love for the man, has become a fear of being without him. Who am I now? I've changed so much of myself to suit Tuck, that I don't know where he ends and I begin. He's taken my choice away now. He's casting me aside for Danielle.

I can see her at one of the tables; they must have met through Teddy. I recognise her from the disgusting pictures I found. As per the usual cliché, she's younger than me. I can't believe her audacity to be here. I have decided to leave after the wedding, I don't want to spoil it for René who has become a good friend to me. She's having her wedding here at Wayne's Texas ranch. It's a popular wedding destination, ensuring a steady roll of income into his already fat pockets. He's old money with a good head for business. I never cared about all that, but he assumes I'll try and fleece him now. All the years I loved him, and he never saw any of it. He doesn't know me. That somehow seems worse than all the affairs. I wanted a loving husband, not a divorce settlement. I wanted to be married, really married. I was, and Tuck wasn't it seems.

The hall is decked out in white taffeta and subtle fairy lights, hanging from the high beamed ceilings of the main ranch building. The rustic tables are blanketed in white,

187

like iced cakes with bouquets of wildflowers arranged in the centre. The beautiful Renée wears a modest, fitted lace dress, with a long train. Her hair is braided in fairy-tale style, with white daisies and pearl beads pinned in all the way down. Her braid falls down her back ending at her bottom. Two hundred of her closest friends and family are here to see them married today. Two hundred people sitting waiting for my soon to be ex-husband's toast and advice on marriage. The irony is unbelievable.

The sharp noise of silver on crystal calms the swell of laughter and chatter across the happy room. The Master of Service introduces Tuck, the best man, for his speech. My eyes find Danielle again, who sparkles with excitement at her table. I looked at him that way once. He begins his speech.

'I met my friend Teddy, way back in junior school and I haven't been able to get rid of him since. I'm the reason this little geek made it out of high school alive,' he says gripping Teddy by the shoulder fondly. Teddy laughs awkwardly behind his glasses, he's probably the only other person that takes as much shit off Tuck as I do.

'But despite his lack of sporting prowess or any sort of sense of humour, I took him under my wing and made him the man he is today,' he continues and the crowd chuckle awkwardly. 'I made him my best friend.'

These naïve suckers swoon at his words.

'And today, the beautiful René has made him a husband,' he says looking at me now. For show he smiles a warm, loving smile and raises his champagne to me.

'With any luck he'll be half as happy as me.'

What a lying piece of shit.

'To toast the lovely couple, I'm going to open a very expensive bottle of whisky and pour Teddy a glass. Many

188

nights I've carried him home after too many scotches, so it seems only appropriate,'

Tuck's pulling his prized bottle out of its box. He fiddles at the neck trying to find the foil to crack it open. As he struggles, I see him beginning to look faint. He begins to address his audience again to kill time, but his words come out in garbled nonsense. We all look alarmed as his face begins to droop at one side. Instinctively, I rush from my table to the top table where Teddy and René are dealing with the situation. His whisky has been taken from him and they are trying to get him to raise his arms as the master of ceremonies phones the ambulance. I reach him and they part to let me in. He looks a poor creature, slumped on the chair. I can tell he's panicking. I scan the room for Danielle, but she's disappeared. I take his hand, although I know he doesn't want me. I board the ambulance with him and wait by his side. Because I loved this man once. And my mamma named me Audrey after Audrey Hepburn. Audrey always said people, even more than things, have to be restored, renewed, revived, reclaimed, and redeemed. Never throw out anyone. If he recovers, our divorce will carry through. For now, we're married, really married.

Chapter 42
The Guru
Barley:

Tuck never recovered. Not fully anyway. Paralysis has left him wheelchair bound and dependent on others. Aphasia prevents him from verbal communication. He relies heavily on Audrey now, who has taken over the company in lieu of his health deterioration. I would like to have seen her break free from his hold, but she seems quite happy now. She's sold me on now that Tuck won't be drinking, and I'm glad I survived the wedding. It was a close call there. At least I left knowing that Audrey is ok, and when Tuck finally goes, she'll get the whole lot and not just the half he planned to give her. I hope he appreciates the kindness she shows him daily. He's spent most of their life together tearing her down. Now he clings to her for support.

I'm on stage at Toronto university, at a Ted Talk event. I'm not speaking at it today, no, I've matured well but they'd have me locked up in some government lab if they knew what was really going on here. My new owner, Matthew Faustaux, is an internationally recognised self-help guru. You think that's bad? Try spending the last two years, touring with him as a prop for his talks and listening to the pish he spouts.

Never a handsomer man was created mind you. I can see why everyone hangs on his every word. He's Canadian and here in his hometown today speaking at his alumni college. He's so 'stoked' as these Canadians like to say. His theories have swept the planet and it seems every man and their granny has subscribed to it. He started on You-tube with a blog and a theory, and now he's gone onto international acclaim and his books are selling out all over the world. It's mad how the world works these days. His philosophy is called 'The Spider' and I can't think of a creepier name to be honest.

Anyway, I'm here on a small desk on stage, with his water bottle perched beside me.

There are hundreds of people in front of me, but luckily the bright lights of the stage block mostly all but the front row out. It's very intimidating being up here. Their eyes are glued to me on the stage. Wondering why there is a bottle of whisky there. The host begins to introduce Matthew.

'Please welcome onto the stage, self-help genius and the author of the best-selling book, *The Spider- A simple Philosophy for happiness*, Matthew Faustaux!' he says with enthusiasm and rallies the crowd to clap. The noise fills the huge lecture theatre. Matthew comes running onto the stage, clutching a shiny copy of his book. He is dressed in a well-fitting suit of powder blue and shiny brown shoes. His curly hair is crunchy with gel and his smile never slips once. He holds the book above his head, as the crowd grows noisier. When they calm doon, to hear what he says, he clutches the book to his chest. All the while the front cover stays faced at them. The intimidating image of a dangerous spider confronts them.

'Most people look at this cover and feel fear,' he says addressing the gruesome creature on the cover. 'Not just the spider guys, but a very scary word. Happiness,' he pauses, allowing the room to take it all in. 'There's nothing more terrifying to most of you out there than happiness,' he says making another bold statement. 'We spend so much time being unhappy, that we don't know what life will be like to experience real happiness. We fear the unknown.

People are afraid to make the simple changes they need to start enjoying their life.' He places the book on the table beside me.

He clicks a small remote at the screen and a basic diagram of a spider appears. Each leg is adorned with ruby writing with the words *Mind, Body, Soul, Positive, Creative, Frugal, Organised,* and *Proactive* upon them.

'It's not hard to be happy, guys. And you shouldn't be afraid of it. With my 8-factor way of living, each one of you can achieve a happier tomorrow,' he boasts, and the crowd begin to clap again. With a knowing smile he nods, until the din has subsided.

'The spider came to me as a natural spirit animal on my way to discovering this theory. The spider weaves its web, putting so much effort into it. Yet when it is destroyed, does the spider give up? No. So why should you give up on your happiness? Look to the wisdom of the humble spider; who weaves a philosophy of happiness for those brave enough to gaze upon its web. By following my eight simple guidelines inspired by the spider, you too can vastly improve your happiness and create the life you dream of.'

I want to vomit. I really don't buy all this self-help garbage. If it really was so easy, then we'd have world peace. Still Matthew batters on.

'The steps are simple! Each day aim to enrich your mind, take care of your body, feed your soul, embrace creativity, be organised, be positive, be proactive and be frugal with your time and energy.'

Pointing to the screen he pulls up the focus words individually. 'First we have creativity. Studies have shown that people who class themselves as creative live longer, better quality lives,' Matthew says, flicking through slides and providing statistics for each point. 'Creative activity has been highlighted as beneficial in lowering blood pressure and to healing from traumatic experiences. Mental health professionals testify to the benefits of exploring creativity for mental health.'

The crowd are in awe of him, and he chats a good game I will admit.

'Psychologists detect a positive correlation between creative pursuits and life satisfaction scores across the board. It's literally boosting people's happiness all over the place,' he says, bouncing on his toes as he explains. He's passionate about his work. Me? I don't think it can apply to everyone. What about those who have no control over their lives all over the world. How can they implement this? It's too idealistic.

'In schools across the country, teachers are noticing a connection between creative outlets and the development of better learning strategies for pupils,' he says in excitement. 'In numerous studies, those given a creative task before problem solving tests achieved significantly higher than those who did no creative task. We are slowly acknowledging that feeding the brain this good energy benefits us greatly. But can you apply it to your life?' Matthew pauses and scans the audience.

'You might feel you don't have a creative bone in your body, but I guarantee there is something in your life you can do. I urge you to find that untapped creativity and use it daily,' he coaches. 'Think on the benefits our lovely spider reaps from creating her web. A place to rest, a net to catch her dinner and a pantry for when times are tough. Your creativity can be all these things to you. A place of solace and respite; a much-needed sustenance for your mind and soul and something to turn to when times are hard.' The crowd applaud his emotive language. He's a showman.

The talk continues and he provides positive evidence for focussing on the other seven areas. He makes emphasis on the power of positivity.

'I'm a great believer in energies. We are energy, we can be broken down into basic atoms. We can tap into that energy,' he begins. 'The power of prayer astounds me, but I don't believe in a higher power,' he says and there is an uncomfortable murmur across the room. 'Instead I believe that we are the higher power. We can achieve wonderful things when we pull our energies together as a community. That's how I believe prayer works,' he strikes boldly. 'Naturally the opposite must be true, and we should also be wary of pooling our negative energies together.' The front row look to their counterparts and nod in approval, as though he's onto something with this. It could have gone either way, challenging organised religion.

'I believe in the balance of the universe. Simply put, the universe will give you everything you ask for. So, if you constantly give out negative thoughts about the world or do negative actions, the universe will keep repaying the favour. It thinks you want the bad. Try instead to put out positive words or actions into the world. You may just find the universe sends you the positive energy you need.' Matthew says as he clicks the screen again to pull up various studies for discussion. Each point he males is neatly summarised with the evidence on the screen, paired with lots of happy real-life people.

'Consistently inducing a positive mood boosts health in terminal patients, improving quality of life,' Matthew says, bringing the study up for the people to see. 'In fact, positive people are scientifically shown to feel less pain in pain induction experiments than those who were more

194

negatively inclined.' With every statement, I can see the crowd swell with support for him. 'Positive people are reported to get more opportunities, not only because people are drawn to them, but their positive mental schemas about the world allow them to see and seize such opportunities.'

Matthew is reaching the home pitch of his talk.

'Children of positive parents consistently outperformed their comparative counterparts in academic tasks and in life satisfaction score across the board. Your level of positivity can even be directly linked to your intrinsic self-worth, so it's crucial for your happiness to address it,' he concludes. The crowd claps throughout, as they do in every city, we've toured over the last few years. Now we come to my part of the show. The anecdote.

'I bring this expensive bottle of malt whisky with me everywhere I go,' he smiles. 'I carry it around like my sins, my chains like Jacob Marley,' he says holding me up to the bright lights and the audience.

'When I reached international success, I invested in the bottle. I love scotch and thought how cool it would be to have this old whisky,' he says, taking a sadder tone now.

'But I can't bring myself to drink it. I just can't,' he says, 'even though I know it will make me happy to taste it.' The crowd gives him sympathy.

'Like me, you all carry about your means to happiness. You know what it is. But you are unwilling to allow yourself to experience it,' says Matthew with passion.

'You deserve not to fear your own happiness. To love yourself a little more,' he rallies and the crowd cheer in response.

'This is my proof that I don't know everything and there's still a lot for me to learn. But living by the spider has certainly changed my life. Maybe it can change yours too.'

The crowd erupt, applause filling the hall as he thanks them and departs. He's a tough act to follow, Matthew. He's an even tougher act to live with.

Chapter 43
Self-medicated
Matthew:

I take another line and the buzz rushes through my body. I dap the blood away from my nostril. Too much for today I think, but I need the energy boost to get through the interview about to happen. Anyone in their right mind would class being interviewed by Ashana as one of the pinnacles of their career. But I'm not in my right mind, and I haven't been for a long time. I need this daily crutch to cope. A chap at the dressing room door tells me it's time for the green room and I wipe away any remnants on the counter with the wipes left by the make-up artist. The mirror reflects a face I barely know anymore. I used to play ice-hockey, sustaining a constant barrage of injuries and living on the adrenaline. Now the only black eyes I see are when my eyeliner starts to sweat. I don't have time for the things I love anymore.

I wait in the green room with the other stars. Being called a star is another thing I've had to get used to. I used to cringe at the words, but eventually you start to half believe the bullshit they feed you. Politics. That's how it all started for me. I've always had the gift of the gab, a natural born communicator. I was head of debates in high school, but my natural ease with people also ensured my popularity. Drama classes were my flair, and I burned through my degree in Politics at Toronto University with no problems. What good was it to chase politics after college though? I couldn't really make a difference in the world, not that way. I worked in office job instead, earning a decent pay because of my qualifications. I started a normal life for myself, an unhappy life. That's where my blog began. I wanted to be happier, and before I knew it my ideas had hurled me into this limelight. I became a politician of sorts, but more of a salesman. I've been selling this recipe for happiness ever since. I've been rewarded with wealth and fame, but its all bullshit. I've never been unhappier. I can't follow my own advice.

'Welcome onto the stage, Matthew Faustaux,' I hear the host, Ashana, say as I make my way through the short hallway and onto the stage. She's this generation's Oprah Winfrey, her talents spanning across all areas of celebrity culture. She greets me warmly with a kiss and handshake and I take a seat on the couch opposite her. I sip on the cucumber water provided, to try and rid myself of dry mouth. Her smile almost falters as she sees my pupils, but she remains as professional as ever. The camera will never pick up on it anyway. I gave up on the eye-drops when I realised that.

'Well, Matthew, it's lovely to see you again,' she says with breezy charm and I return the favour and compliment how well she looks. These TV gigs are usually just small talk on steroids. We've met in passing at a friend's event.

'We're so intrigued to hear about your upcoming trip to Tibet!' she says, including the audience who clap their hands in excitement. 'Can you tell us a little more about that?'

I laugh, beaming my signature smile out to the audience.

'Sure thing,' I say, crossing my leg over my knee and holding it in place. 'I'm going in preparation for my next book, *Beyond the Spider*,' I say and the audience gurgles with loud whoops and whistles. It's flattering, but they don't know the next book consists of three lines. So far, they all say, *Fuck you, Michael!* Michael is my editor by the way, and he's threatening to swipe the deal away if I don't meet the looming deadline. I'm screwed, but Ashana certainly doesn't want to hear that. No one wants to know how you're really coping.

'Thanks!' I say, with a modest smile, brushing their flattery away with my hand. 'It takes a closer look at philosophy for happiness and enlightenment across cultures, to see what we can learn from them. Understandably, I'm keen to go to Tibet, a global hotspot for enlightenment.' Ashana looks relieved that I'm not too out of my head to give up the goods in the interview.

'Sounds fabulous,' she enthuses. 'Am I right in saying you are actually having an audience with the Dalai Lama?'

'That's correct,' I say with excitement, and it's the only thing that's not false about this interview. I'm honoured to meet her, the first re-incarnation of the Dalai Lama to be female. I hope that my trip to Tibet can help me spiritually. I don't have anyone to talk to, if I do, I reveal myself as a fraud and the whole empire I've created comes tumbling down. I'm trapped by my own achievements. My self-help has turned to self-medication. 'I have been granted an audience with her and I've never been more honoured in my life,' I say genuinely. I can see the audience is craving the cheese they came here for, 'except for meeting with you today Ashana!' I charm, and everyone seems quite happy with my effort.

After a few more questions, the interview concludes and I wait on the couch as more stars appear. I interact with them in the usual witty banter. I'm already thinking of my next line and praying that Tibet can free me.

Chapter 44
Spirited Away
Barley:

Matthew presented me to the Dalai Lama at a meeting crawling with global television reporters. He wanted to use me as a symbol of seeking true happiness by shunning the allure of physical possessions. After their meeting, he donated almost all his assets to charities around the world and decided to patch the next book in favour of travelling the world. The public thought he'd had a mental breakdown, but I like to think maybe he's found happiness somewhere under a coconut tree. Hopefully he's stopped shoving that horrible stuff up his snib. That's no way to live.

The female Dalai Lama accepted the gift graciously and I have lived in her quarters here, in Tibet, ever since. I have sunk happily into a life of quiet contemplation and appreciation of simple living. It isn't a wild party here every night, but there is a sense of safety and an intrinsic feeling of wellbeing about the place. That was until one of her female guardian's took a shine to me. She's been eyeing me up for months, taking special care to read my box as she meticulously cleans the living quarters. Slowly, over the months I've been here, she's been stealing away artefacts from the Dalai Lama's quarters and selling them on. She's chosen today to strike.

Before she places me in her satchel, she begins lighting the meditation incense in preparation for the Dalai Lama's return from her trek. Her shift is over now, and if she is lucky, Hana will be blamed for the theft. Amala is the known favourite after all, so it's unlikely she will be suspected. She lights the sticks, and I inhale the warm spice. She reaches up to my perch and places me into her satchel. I say cheerio to the twin Tibetan singing bowls that had stood century at my side. They sing in reply, but only I can hear it. If I could, I'd rattle the beaters in protest and tell someone about this wee thief. I don't want to leave here, who knows where I'll end up. She turns in greedy excitement and tries to scarper from the room. Knowing eyes stop her in her tracks.

'Your holiness, I—' she manages to squeak out as she pulls me free from the satchel again. She looks up in guilt at the woman she cares for daily. She is considered a living Buddha in Tibetan culture, and a reincarnation of all the Lamas before her. Their wisdom is said to pass though the generations. The Dalai Lama raises her hand, not in anger, but to halt Amala. She takes me in her hands and looks soulfully into her guardian's eyes, before placing me back into the satchel upon her shoulders.

'Anything I have, I readily share with my friends,' she says looking at Amala with kindness. 'I only ask that you extend such kindness to me.' Amala looks mortified and hangs her head in shame. A small kiss on her forehead and cool hands on her shoulders bring forgiveness.

'Your shift has ended, Amala. You may go.'

Amala almost runs from the room, clutching me in the safety of the satchel. Where I will go next I don't know. You never can trust a thief.

Chapter 45

Harmony

Barley:

What a journey I've had. I've been passed from shady dealer to shady dealer. None of them knew my true value and often were just trying to get rid of me as fast as possible. I was stolen from the living buddha; the Dalai lama in Tibet. I passed through Tibet, Russia, Norway and finally went to Sweden where someone knew what they were doing. I was later bought at auction by the owner of this pub, the *Harmony Inn*. I'm glad to be back on home soil, just up the road from the distillery, in Glasgow. At least it feels a bit more like home. The auld yin that bought me is actually alright to be fair. He's full of the patter and he's put me up in one of the best spots on the gantry. What a gantry it is by the way. It's like Aladdin's cave for bevvy. Mirrored glass shelves adorn it, glittering under spotlights and showcasing over 500 malt whiskies. That's not even mentioning all the other spirits here. Aye, there are worse places to be than this wee boozer. I've ruffled a few feathers by being here.

The other whiskies pelter me, because they think I act like I'm better than them. Actually, they're probably right, because I do think that. I've done hard time in the barrel. I never got released early and rattled out to be bottled ten a penny. I tried to make pals with the oldest whisky on the bar, a 70-year-old from Speyside. He's having none of it though and sits sneering down at me from the top shelf. He's giving me a hard time right now. Listen.

'You'll never reach such dizzying heights,' he says as one of the bar staff clean the shelf he sits on. 'You'll never be top dog here.'

I don't care anyway; I don't want to be his mate. I'm sick of having to shout to have a conversation with him. He's too auld to hear me properly. I don't care about being the best either. That's not what it's all about. It's about being the best version of yourself, and I'm doing a smashing job of that. Anyway, the only gaffer in here is my big mate Paul. He's a hard worker; in here knocking his pan in every day. He's a generous man who collects lots for charities and true gentleman to anyone in need. He goes the extra mile for his customers and that's why they all look at this place as their local, even if they live nowhere near it. The Harmony is their home from home. I just wish he'd shift some of these cheeky whiskies.

'Alright, Barley!' I hear the beautiful pink gin beside me say. That's my wee sweetheart, Blossom, she's stunning. Normally the gins are segregated to a different area, politics, but because she's so popular she's on an optic right beside my shelf.

'How ye doing Blossom, doll?' I say, pattering her up. I notice that her level is getting dangerously low. She's not got long left. I don't know what I'll do without her here. She keeps me going.

'All the better for seeing you, love,' she sings to me cheerily and brightens my day, as always. I love her. From the top of her optic to the Japanese writing on her base. I wish that someone would make an expensive cocktail with us, so we could mingle together in a glass. For now, we must love from a far.

In the time I've been here, I've been taken down and inspected a million times. The grubby fingerprints of prospective customers are polished off my body after the disappointment. The nonsense I must endure with amateurs saying I'm no worth the money, is unreal. Surely a whisky is meant to be drank? For now, I just spend my days with my wee sweetheart and pray that goodbye doesn't come too soon.

Chapter 46
An Old Friend
Barley:

With Blossom gone, I'm all alone and the grief of her passing makes life here unbearable. Just when I'm contemplating shimmying myself off this shelf and to my grave, I hear a familiar voice. It's older now, but still the unmistakable twang of an old friend, someone I've not seen in a very long time. Archie! Archie's just walked into the bar and I'd know him no matter how many years have passed. Though he must be about 70 now and wrinkles dominate his face I can still see those eyes twinkle. He's got his grandson with him, who's shouting the pints up. They sit at the far end of the bar and admire all the bottles. Archie, do you no see me? It's me, Barley!

Archie sups down a pint of Deuchars and chats to Paul.

'Is that an Ionach you've got there?' Archie says, squinting his eyes at me. He wears big bottle glasses now, as I guess that time has taken its toll on his sight. I see him clear as day.

'Aye, I've a few actually. Cracking distillery,' says big Paul enthusiastically. 'It's only up the road and it's one of the only few I've not been to. I've always been meaning to book a tour.'

'I'll sort ye out nae bother,' Archie says, reaching into his smart jacket and fishing out a business card. He slides it over to Paul, who looks delighted, as they shake hands and introduce themselves.

'This is the Barley Cask, 44 years,' he says climbing the tall ladder to reach me. He sets me down in front of Archie.

I can't believe this is real. I love ye Archie, I'm so glad you're here.

Up close now, I see how the years have ravaged my auld mate. He reads me clearly now through his bi-focals. The smile that bursts onto his face makes me feel like I'm home. I've missed ye Archie. You don't know the things I've been through, the stuff I've seen. At least now you're here, ye can take me home, like you always said.

'You know,' Archie says handing me back to Paul, 'that cask was the very first whisky I ever produced believe it or not.'

Aye we know Archie, I'm unique. Get a price for me, don't leave me hanging here anymore. What's happening here? Don't put me back on the shelf.

I'm put back up on the shelf, raging, and they carry on chatting about whisky. What? No even ordering a dram? No taking me out of this place? Archie, what are ye doing to me? All the hope I ever had of going home leaves as Archie and his grandson walk oot the door a while later to catch the afternoon show at the King's Theatre. He knows I'm here and he doesn't care. I've never felt so worthless in all my life. So much for friendship.

I sink back into stony silence, as the other whiskies take their chance to revel in my misery.

'Oh Archie! Please, come back, I'm so lonely,' whines Laphroaig 10 years, and I hope he falls on his heid and smashes all over the bar floor. I don't even bother replying. Naebody likes Laphroaig anyway, he's a twat. What's the point?

The sleepy afternoon turns into night and I sit stagnant as the pub bursts at the seams with punters. I'm just about to shut my eyes for the night when the door flies open, and the cold Glasgow air enters the bar. I shiver, not only from the cold, but because I have heard the voice of a ghost. Archie is back. His grandson is practically propping him up, they must have done a wee tour of the pubs on the way back from the theatre. Paul is sitting at the other end of the bar, off duty now and chatting with customers.

'How ye doin, pal?' he greets them and shouts them up a drink.

'You know, I've been thinking about that whisky aw day,' confesses Archie, sipping his pint. 'I just couldn't walk away and leave it sitting in this pub. Is there any way I can buy the bottle off ye? It would mean the world to me.'

'Nae bother at all,' says Paul knowingly, and before I know it, I'm taken off the bar and into the safety of the office. They arrange for me to be paid for and picked up tomorrow. Finally, I'm going home.

Chapter 47
Making a Difference
Barley:

We're all sitting around Archie and Alice's dinner table, celebrating the auld yin's 70th. I can see wee Annie here and her man Max, along with all her kids. They're all grown up now with weans of their own. Even Archie's great grand-weans dote on him, every one of them is the spit of him. We sit around a meal made from Enid's recipes and Arthur's prized whisky glasses sit in the middle of the table. We're all here. It's great to be home, surrounded by family. I just sit pride of place at Archie's side and bask in it all. I think every whisky hopes to make a difference in the world. Sitting here I know I have. This distillery and I have brought a family together; and family means everything.

After the meal, Archie reaches into the centre of the table and pulls all the whisky glasses towards him.

'I'd like to do a wee toast. I'm 70 today, and there's no place I'd rather be than here with all my family around me,' he says softly, his voice brimming with emotion. 'I'm a lucky man.'

Archie is peeling the foil away from my lid and suddenly the cork is lifted from my neck with a big pop. It feels like I can breathe for the first time. This is amazing! Archie pours me into several glasses and hands me oot around the table to those old enough to drink. The weans get treated to a spicy cider in their glass to be part of the fun.

'I'd like to raise a glass to those who cannot be with us today to celebrate,' he says, 'and to my wee wife Alice, who has kept me going all these years.'

I see Alice well up. Although the years have eventually aged her too, she'll always be gorgeous to me. She's still got all her own teeth, so that smile hasn't changed a bit.

'I'd also like to toast to Annie, my wee superstar who makes me proud every single day,' he says and Annie beams at her dad across the table. Max squeezes her hand, fondly.

'To family old and new,' he says to his son in law, knowingly. 'To grand weans and great- grand weans taking oor generations forward.'

Archie's chest swells, as he looks at them all.

'And to the whisky that started it all. The Barley Cask, to which I owe my family. If I could live another 70 years, I couldn't be any happier. I wish the same for everyone of ye. I love ye all!' he says as they raise their glasses in cheers.

'Slàinte mhath!' says Archie as they sip from their drams. He swirls me around the glass and admires my legs. Haud oan a wee minute! What's going on here? He's not actually going to drink me. Not his old mate, Barley! He bloody is as well. His big snib is invading the glass now and sniffing up all my delicious aromas.

Citrus of freshly squeezed orange juice in the morning. Toffee stolen from Da's sweetie tin. Milk chocolate shared with the weans on movie nights. Wafts of grassy air from oor field and the memory of kissing Alice behind the stables. Clotted cream from Granny's scones and vanilla birthday cake from Ma. Smokey bacon on a Sunday morning and a thousand memories in the glass.

Hawl you, get those lips away from me ye big bastard! Och, who am I kidding? Slàinte mhath, Archie mate. It's been an absolute pleasure.

Acknowledgements

I'd like to thank my dad, Paul, the person whose idea inspired this novel. I am ever grateful for the love and support he has shown me throughout my life. I wrote this book for his 60th birthday. I wish I could have him by my side for another 60 years. In the event he doesn't live to 120, I know regardless, he'll be with me always. He'll be in my daily thoughts and actions - a guiding presence in my life and there in the person he has helped me to become. He's ever my hero, and the best dad a girl could wish for. So, thank you, Dad. Happy Birthday.

Printed in Great Britain
by Amazon